Richmond upon Thames Libraries

Renew online at www.richmond.gov.uk/libraries

LONDON BOROUGH OF
RICHMOND UPON THAMES

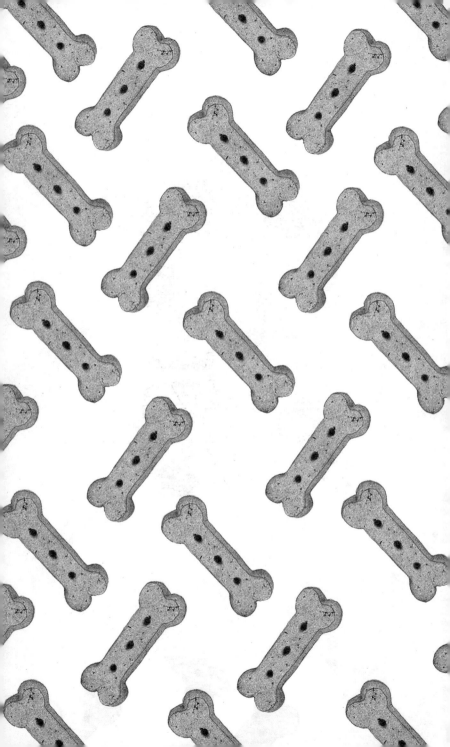

THE INCREDIBLE SHRINKING GIRL Definitely NEEDS A DOG

LOU KUENZLER was brought up on a remote sheep farm on the edge of Dartmoor. After a childhood of sheep, ponies, chickens and dogs, Lou moved to Northern Ireland to study theatre. She went on to work professionally as a theatre director, university drama lecturer and workshop leader in communities, schools and colleges. Lou now teaches adults and children how to write stories and is lucky enough to write her own books, too. She has written children's rhymes, plays and novels as well as stories for CBeebies. Lou lives in London with her family, two cats and a dog.

www.loukuenzler.com

THE INCREDIBLE SHRINKING GIRL Definitely NEEDS A DOG

LOU KUENZLER

Illustrated by Kirsten Collier

SCHOLASTIC

To Duesi because you DEFINITELY
love that dog! LK

Scholastic Children's Books
An imprint of Scholastic Ltd
Euston House, 24 Eversholt Street, London, NW1 1DB, UK
Registered office: Westfield Road, Southam, Warwickshire, CV47 0RA
SCHOLASTIC and associated logos are trademarks and/or
registered trademarks of Scholastic Inc.

First published in the UK as *Shrinking Violet Definitely Needs a Dog*
by Scholastic Ltd, 2013
This edition published 2018

Text copyright © Lou Kuenzler, 2013
Cover illustrations © Risa Rodil, 2018
Inside illustrations copyright © Kirsten Collier, 2013

The right of Lou Kuenzler and Kirstin Collier to be identified as the
author and illustrator of this work has been asserted by them.

ISBN 978 1407 18152 3

A CIP catalogue record for this book
is available from the British Library.

CHAPTER 1

My name is Violet Potts.

This story begins as I was being **VERY** responsible and helping with the washing up.

"See?" I said, scraping a YUCKY lump of spinach stew into the recycling bin. "This family **DEFINITELY** needs a dog!"

I'd been saying this for weeks – ever since my Uncle Max helped me raise enough money to adopt an endangered Siberian wolf cub. I didn't actually get to keep the wolf cub, of course. He had to stay in the frozen forests of Siberia. But I did get a cuddly wolf cub toy and a framed certificate saying:

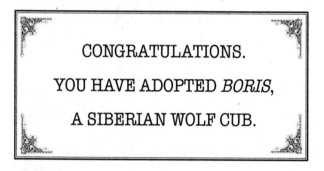

CONGRATULATIONS.
YOU HAVE ADOPTED *BORIS*,
A SIBERIAN WOLF CUB.

Uncle Max is the COOLEST, most BRILLIANT uncle in the whole world, but even he can't get me a real wolf to keep. (Boris wouldn't like to live in our small terrace house at Number 25, King's Park Road – especially as I don't even have my own bedroom. He'd have to share with Tiffany, my terrible teenage sister, too.) But – and here's the really EXCITING bit – Uncle Max did say he might, possibly, perhaps one day get me a puppy.

All I have to do is convince Mum and Dad to agree.

"A dog would definitely eat up all these lovely, yummy leftovers," I said, scraping another plate of sloppy spinach into the bin.

Of course, there is nothing lovely or yummy about spinach stew – it is the **HEALTHIEST**, *SOGGIEST*, **GREENEST** meal of all the healthy, soggy, green meals Mum cooks. But being nice about Mum's cooking was all part of my brilliant plan to make her say yes to a dog.

"No!" said Mum (just as firmly as the four zillion other times she had already said **NO!** that week). "We are **NOT** getting a dog!"

"If Violet gets a dog, I should get new hair straighteners," said Tiffany.

I stared at her with my mouth open. What

did HAIR STRAIGHTENERS have to do with anything? Tiffany is always thinking about her hair. If she was offered the very last seat on the very last lifeboat of a sinking ship, she'd stop to straighten her hair first.

"Honestly," I said. "You're the only person who minds if your hair is frizzy—"

"It isn't FRIZZY!" shrieked Tiffany.

"But a dog would be for the whole family," I carried on. "We could all get fit and healthy taking it for walks." I smiled at Mum. She is very keen on us being fit and healthy.

"If Violet's getting a dog and Tiff's getting hair thingies," grinned Dad, "I should get that new Future Screen TV with the inbuilt 749XG memory chip." I had NO idea what he was talking about, but Dad loves gadgets and technology (almost as much as Mum loves organic vegetables and Tiffany loves her hair).

"Violet is not getting a dog," repeated Mum.

"She wouldn't look after it, anyway," said Tiffany. "She ruined my best black top when I lent it to her for Halloween!"

"Not this again," I groaned. "It's spring. Halloween was months ago. How was I supposed to know Riley Paterson would throw a pot of bogey-green paint at me?"

"Because you two are always fighting," said Tiffany.

This is true. Riley Paterson is the meanest boy in my whole class. He put a frog in my best friend Nisha's witch hat, so I might have known he'd have something horrible planned for me. I should **NEVER** have said trick instead of treat. But I wasn't going tell Tiffany she was right.

"You're so irresponsible, Violet," she huffed. "If you can't even look after a T-shirt, how could you look after a dog?"

"It's not the same thing," I said. "You can't love a T-shirt."

"I can," sighed Tiffany.

"A T-shirt isn't **ALIVE**," I said. "It doesn't go for walks or play fetch." I spun round and shook a sticky spinach spoon at her. "A T-shirt can't bark at burglars or... Whoops! Look out, Tiff!"

A blob of spinach shot off the end of the spoon. It flew through the air and landed, **plop**, on the front of Tiffany's new favourite T-shirt. It was white.

Except now there was a big green $\mathcal{SPLAT}$ of spinach right in the middle.

"I'm so sorry!" I cried. The spinach was *EXACTLY* the same colour as the bogey-green Halloween paint.

"Gross!" screamed Tiffany.

"Careful," shouted Mum as I tossed the spoon into the sink. Another blob of spinach flew through the air. It landed $\mathcal{SQUELCH}$ on the wall and dribbled slowly down into the hamster cage on the counter below.

Hannibal, my podgy hamster, leapt up and stared at me through the bars. Green spinach was dripping off his ears.

"See," said Tiffany. "Violet can't even be trusted with a hamster."

"Or with a spoon," laughed Dad, who always makes jokes at the wrong time.

Mum shot him a look. "Better check the messages on my phone," he said and hurried out of the room.

I tried to follow, but Mum spun round. "Honestly, Violet. Tiffany's right. You really do need to show more responsibility. How could you control a dog if you can't even control yourself?"

"It was an accident," I mumbled as Tiffany stormed past me to go and change her T-shirt. My heart was pounding. Operation Get a Dog was NOT going well.

"I really can be responsible," I said. "I'll show you. I promise."

"You can make a start by getting on with your homework," said Mum, scrubbing at the spinach stain on the wall.

I had a long list of ~~turrifically~~ terrifically ~~tuff~~ tough ~~speelings~~ spellings to learn for the next day.

"I'll test you in a minute," said Mum.

Oh dear. I knew n-e-c-e-s-s-a-r-y was a bit wobbly and Mum would make me write it out ten times if I got it wrong.

Luckily, Dad saved me.

"Come and see this text, Josie," he said, calling

9

to Mum from the lounge. "Max wants to visit. He says he has some wonderful news for us."

"Uncle Max?" I pricked up my ears. "Wonderful news? I – I think that might be to do with me."

"Homework, Violet," said Mum firmly as she left the room.

But I couldn't think about spellings any more.

Uncle Max was coming to visit. He had **WONDERFUL NEWS**? Could it be? I didn't dare to hope. . . But might it be. . .? A dog! My dog!

Excitement bubbled inside me like a fizzy drink. Even my toes started to tingle.

"Uh oh."

I felt a dizzy feeling in my head, as if I were spinning on a fairground waltzer.

I grabbed the edge of the kitchen table, sending a pile of clean cutlery ⚡clattering⚡ to the floor. I tried to steady myself. But it was too late.

"Violet will be thrilled," I heard Mum say from the lounge.

And that was it.

WHOOSH!

I was shrinking . . . **FAST!**

CHAPTER 2

"WHOO!"

I was shrinking so quickly it felt like I was riding a roller coaster – which is funny because the very first time I ever shrank I was in the queue at a theme park. One minute I was a normal ten-year-old girl, TALL enough to ride on PLUNGER!, my dream roller coaster. The next minute, by the time I reached the measuring stick, POP! I was no bigger than a frozen fish finger.

I've shrunk lots of times since then and it always

starts with the same tiny tingling in my toes.

WHOOSH. And I'm plunging towards the floor.

"Whoa!" I cried now as the top of the kitchen table, a shelf of cookery books and the legs of a chair whizzed past.

CLANG!

I landed amongst the cutlery I had knocked to the floor.

"Ouch!" The sharp prongs of one of the forks poked me in the bum as if I were a juicy meatball. I rolled over next to a silver teaspoon the same size as me.

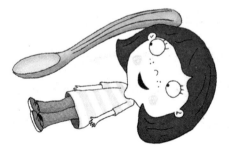

I rubbed my sore bum and lay beside the teaspoon. We were like two tiny patients in a row of hospital beds.

"What are you here for? A bent handle?" I giggled.

At least no one else was in the kitchen. I was worried Mum might have heard the clatter of cutlery and come to see what was going on.

She has **NO** idea that I sometimes shrink. No one in my family does. Except Gran – she used to be a shrinker too, when she was a girl. She says the world's not ready for our little secret yet. I think she's right.

I did try and tell Mum and Dad what had happened when I shrank that first time at the theme park. They just got cross and said I was making it up.

But I'm not making it up. Whenever I get

overexcited, WHOOSH! I shrink to the size of a lollipop.

No wonder I shrank this time, I thought as I crawled out from the cutlery. *What could be more* EXCITING *than Uncle Max coming to visit? Especially if he might really, truly bring me a puppy of my own.*

Could this be THE LUCKY VISIT? With Uncle Max's help, would Mum and Dad finally agree?

If only I could get to the lounge and hear what they were saying.

Just one small problem. Moving around a house isn't easy when you are the size of a teaspoon. I would have to heave myself up the steps in the corridor like a mini mountaineer.

Luckily, Tiffany had dropped one of her

sparkly earrings on the carpet. It was her favourite – a silver moon. She'd be glad that I'd found it. It might even make up for the soggy spinach on her T-shirt. But for now, I dug the sharp stud into the stairs and used it as a tiny pickaxe to pull myself up. I clung to it like one of those sharp pointy tools climbers stick into the rocks and ice.

AWESOME! My legs dangled beneath me as if I were hanging from a real precipice like the ones I've seen on my favourite TV show: **EXPLORE GALORE!**

"Here I am in the frozen mountains," I whispered, pretending I was Stella Lightfoot, the super-cool presenter who is always jumping out of helicopters and scrambling over rocks. I imagined I had my own mini camera crew following me as I climbed Mount Corridor-Steps.

"What a view," I giggled, wishing my best friend, Nisha, could be here – she loves playing imaginary games and she thinks Stella Lightfoot is really pretty.

Of course, if Nisha were here, I'd have to hide from her too. Even though she's my best friend, she has no idea about my shrinking either.

Maybe we could play a Stella Lightfoot game when I grew back to full size. Maybe I would even have my own puppy by then. Maybe we could pretend it was a husky dog to pull us through the snow. Maybe... But I was getting carried away.

For now, I had to get to the lounge and find

out what Mum and Dad were saying.

"On through the GREAT white wilderness," I smiled as I trekked across the fluffy carpet in the hall. Taking one tiny step after another, I made my way towards the lounge door. As I got closer, I could hear Dad talking.

It took me a moment to realize he must be on the phone.

"Wonderful. . . That's great news, Max," he said. "Yes. . . Josie and I are both very excited. . . Of course, not a word. See you Saturday. Bye. . ."

Through the crack in the open door, I saw Dad put his mobile phone on the coffee table.

"So?" said Mum. "What did Max say?" She sounded excited.

But Dad put his finger to his lips. "Best not to be overheard," he said. "Let me close the door."

I made a dash forward. If I could sneak into the room and hide under the sofa, I could hear what they were going to say. But I was too late. Dad stepped forward and. . .

"Yikes!" I jumped backwards and rolled away across the hall carpet as he closed the door between us.

"Phew!" Just in time. Dad hadn't seen me down here, of course. But if he'd slammed the door on me, I'd have been squashed flat as a biscuit.

"Max wants to keep everything secret," I heard him say, from inside the lounge. Then his voice dropped to a whisper.

I knew I shouldn't be listening, but it was like peeking in the wardrobe where Mum and Dad hide the Christmas presents. I just couldn't ~sist. . .

CHAPTER 3

If I had been just a centimetre smaller, I might have been able to wriggle underneath the lounge door. Instead, I was stuck in the hall, with my ear pressed against the wood. I couldn't catch half of what Dad was saying, just the odd whispered word. It was like trying to listen to a radio when it's not properly tuned in.

"hhh 〰 adorable 〰 hhh 〰 if we agree hhh 〰 surprise for Violet hh〰 tell her himself when he comes hhh 〰 "

"But that's lovely," said Mum. She really did sound pleased. Did that mean she had agreed with Uncle Max's suggestion?

I couldn't catch the rest of what she was saying either.

"hhh ᳕᳝ big responsibility"

I heard footsteps and the door handle turned above me. Quick as a mouse, I scampered across the hall and shot behind the umbrella stand.

As Mum and Dad came out of the lounge, I crouched in the shadows trying to make sense of what I had heard.

Uncle Max had a surprise. A surprise for me. It was something adorable ... but also a big responsibility. Surely that could only mean ONE wonderful, WAGGY-TAILED thing?

It was all I could do not to leap up and down

and cheer. I was doing a secret, silent mini tap dance of **JOY** when the letter box on the front door rattled above me.

I strained my neck to look up as a leaflet shot through the slot, floated over the umbrella stand and drifted past my head. It was an advertisement of some kind. There was a picture of a cute tabby kitten and a gorgeous black and white sheepdog puppy with a plaster on its leg.

For a second, I thought I must be dreaming. But there it was, floating through the air! A picture of a puppy at the **EXACT** moment I was thinking about my very own dog. Was this some kind of **BRILLIANT**, *spooky*, MAGIC sign?

As the advert landed on the doormat, I peered round the edge of the umbrella stand and read the big blue writing on the front:

"What's that?" said Dad, as Mum stepped forward to pick up the leaflet.

I jumped back into the shadows.

"Something about helping to walk rescue dogs," she said, glancing at the paper.

"Better not let Violet see that," laughed Dad. "She'll want to adopt them all."

"She'll be too busy. Her hands will be full in the next few weeks," said Mum. She opened the front door and tossed the advert outside into the paper recycling bin. "It's junk mail. We don't need it."

What did she mean, my hands would be full? With what? I felt a **HUGE** grin spread across my tiny face.

There was a jolt in my neck. I realized it wasn't just my smile that was growing big. . .

POP!

I shot back to full size, sending umbrellas tumbling like pick-up sticks across the hall.

"Violet!" screamed Mum, leaping into the air. "What are you doing there?"

"Nothing," I mumbled, poking my head out from behind Dad's raincoat. I had shot up in amongst the coat rack as I grew. It's one of the strange things about shrinking: I never know when I'm going to grow back to full size. Now my left foot was stuck in the umbrella stand.

"You didn't half make me jump," gasped Dad, who was nearly at the top of the stairs. "Were you hiding?"

"Er ... no," I said as Mum shut the front door. I noticed my book bag hanging on the peg beside Dad's raincoat. "I was just ... er ... checking if I had any extra spellings. But I don't ... so I'll get ready for bed now."

I squeezed past Dad and charged up the stairs before they could ask me any more questions.

By the time Mum came to check on me, I was tucked up reading my **Bumper Book Of Dogs**. I had already put my clothes in the laundry bin, brushed my teeth and washed behind my ears. I had to do everything I could to show Mum and Dad that I was totally, completely responsible enough to look after a puppy the moment it arrived.

The really **TRICKY** thing was making sure I didn't get overexcited and shrink again in the next few days. Nobody would **EVER** let me get a dog if they discovered I'm sometimes small enough to be gobbled up like a treat. I wasn't worried about that, though – I knew I'd be able to train my puppy the minute we met.

Every time Mum and Dad mentioned Uncle Max's visit over the next few days I had to pinch myself and think of something horrible like spelling tests or being desperate for the loo when Tiffany's hogging the bathroom. It wasn't easy. Mum and Dad kept dropping hints, saying I was going to get a lovely surprise and winking at each other.

By breakfast on Saturday, I couldn't stand it any longer. It was the day of Uncle Max's visit.

"Give me one little clue about the surprise," I begged.

Dad looked up from fiddling with the new fancy toaster he had bought. It was supposed to make *PERFECT* toast. At the moment, all it was doing was shooting out slices of burnt black charcoal every two minutes.

"Here's a good clue," he said, fanning away a plume of thick grey smoke. He started to sing a funny little tune. "Da da dada. Da da dada. . ."

Dad is always REALLY off key, so this was hopeless.

"You look like you can't make head nor tail of it," he chuckled.

"Head nor tail?" Was that another clue? My heart was pounding. "Is it 'How Much Is That Doggy in the Window'?" I tried.

"Nope." Dad was grinning from ear to ear . . . until the smoke alarm starting SCREECHING and he had to climb on a chair to switch it off.

"Mum? Give me a proper clue," I shouted over the blaring alarm. "No singing!"

"OK." Mum paused with a slice of grapefruit

halfway to her mouth. "I know. . . There'll be two of you."

"And a bit of a walk," smiled Dad, climbing down from the chair.

Two of us? Walking? I grabbed a slice of charcoal-black toast. I was hoping the taste of something horrible would stop me getting overexcited. I sprinkled pepper all over the top of it, too.

"Violet?" said Mum. "What are you doing? You've been acting very strangely lately."

"Just . . . eating breakfast," I said truthfully as I took a **BIG** burnt, peppery bite.

I couldn't shrink.

Not now.

Uncle Max would be here in less than two hours!

CHAPTER 4

As soon as breakfast was over, I sat in the front window waiting.

Necessary I wrote in my notepad (I had got the spelling wrong in my test last week, so it was back on the list again).

Participate.

I have **NEVER** practised my spellings so many times, but it was a brilliant, boring way to make sure I didn't shrink.

I'm always excited when Uncle Max comes to

visit – it had been a month since I had seen him, at least. Although he is Dad's little brother, they are nothing alike. Uncle Max is a total daredevil. I call him **SUPER MAX!** He writes travel books and he's been on **WILD** and **DANGEROUS** trips around the world – he's probably been to even more cool places than a wild celebrity adventurer like Stella Lightfoot.

Whenever he's here, we always do something *AWESOME*. Last time we made a home-made splurge gun and he took me paintballing in the woods. The time before was when we had the sponsored jumpathon on Nisha's trampoline. **SUPER MAX** kept bouncing until midnight so that we would raise enough money to adopt Boris, the endangered wolf cub.

"That'll have to keep you going until I'm

allowed to get you a real dog," he'd laughed on the phone, when the certificate and stuffed toy had arrived.

Courageous I wrote as a car turned into our street. I looked up, hoping it would be Uncle Max's battered green jeep. But it wasn't. It was a shiny blue car. It looked brand new. Not a speck of dust anywhere. A little toy lamb was swinging from the mirror in the front windscreen.

I smiled to myself and turned back to my spellings.

Uncle Max would never drive a car like that. His jeep has a big plastic bat hanging from the mirror. It doesn't even have any doors – just bits of green canvas. He wears a crazy driving hat with corks hanging off it that he brought back from Australia.

Unusual, I wrote.

I glanced up.

The blue car was stopping outside our house.

The driver got out. Probably going next door.

I giggled to myself as I noticed he was wearing a

pale blue suit EXACTLY the same colour as the

shiny car.

A woman in a matching blue dress climbed out of the passenger side.

The driver turned around and took a step towards our house.

I gasped. "Uncle Max?" My eyes nearly popped out of my head.

But it couldn't be him. . . Surely not? This man was the same height as Uncle Max. He had the same crooked nose, where he'd broken it falling off an elephant in India. The same sandy blond hair. . . But instead of a long shaggy mop, it was cut short and neat, oiled flat against his head. His wild beard was gone too, leaving a small, thin moustache . . . and he was wearing a flowery pink tie.

"Goodness," said Mum, who had come up behind me and was peering over my shoulder. "Doesn't Max look smart?"

She tapped the window. **"Hello!"**

Uncle Max looked up and waved. The shiny blue woman waved too. She was very short with big FLUFFY blonde hair and she wobbled on a pair of very TALL, very shiny blue high-heeled shoes. She squeezed Max's arm and giggled.

"That must be Bunny," said Mum. "Max's special lady."

Special lady? What did that mean?

"Max was right," cooed Mum. "She is adorable. Come on, Violet. Let's go and say hello."

"Adorable?" I stared out of the window with my mouth wide open.

As Mum went to the door, I stood on tiptoe to take a better look at the parked car outside. There didn't seem to be any sign of a puppy . . . not even a muddy paw print on the pale blue leather seats.

"Come on in," said Mum, in the hall.

I heard a tinkly laugh which must have been Bunny's and that strange lip-sucking noise grown-ups make when they kiss each other in mid-air.

"Violet!" cried Uncle Max, bounding into the lounge. "There you are."

He charged forward with his hand raised ready for a high five.

"Wow, Maxi. You're so good with kids," giggled Bunny, clip-clopping in behind him. Mum, Dad and Tiffany followed her.

"Oh, not really." Uncle Max looked at Bunny and blushed. He dropped his hand and straightened his tie as if he hadn't been planning on doing a high five at all.

"Er . . . have you been working hard at school, Violet?" he said.

"WORKING HARD AT SCHOOL?"

I punched him playfully in the stomach. "Honestly, Uncle Max. What sort of question is that?"

Tiffany sniggered.

"School is very important! You can ... well, you can learn all sorts of lessons there," said Bunny. She grabbed me by both hands. "But I am not going to be strict Auntie Bunny. You and I shall be great friends."

Auntie Bunny? Who did she think she was? I'd only met her a few seconds ago.

"I don't have any aunties," I said.

"Not yet," she giggled and pinched my cheek. "Maxi told me you were cute."

Cute? I stuck out my chin and put my hands on my hips.

"Really cute," said Bunny, sounding a little less

sure. "That's why we've got a big surprise for you. Haven't we, Maxi, my sweet?"

"Yes?" Uncle Max nodded his head. He looked like one of those silly wobbly toy dogs people have in the back of their cars.

"A surprise?" I said. My fingers were crossed tight behind my back. Uncle Max didn't actually have a puppy with him, but perhaps we were all going to pile into the pale blue car and drive to a kennel somewhere. Perhaps it was a rescue pup from the

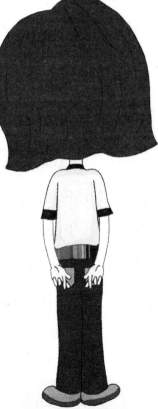

PAW THINGS

animal charity, like I'd seen on

the leaflet. That was just the sort of thing Uncle Max would do.

"It's a very special surprise," said Mum.

"You see, Bunny is my fiancée," said Uncle Max.

"Wow! Congratulations!" screamed Tiffany, jumping up and down as if it was the most exciting thing she had ever heard.

Mum beamed. "We're so pleased for you both."

"Lucky man, Max," winked Dad.

"Fiancée?" I gasped.

"It means they're engaged," said Tiffany. "They're going to get married, stupid."

"I know what fiancée means," I said.

"Da da dada! Da da dada," sang Dad. And, as everyone else joined in, I recognized the wedding tune.

"And. . ." said Uncle Max.

"We want you to be our bridesmaid," grinned Bunny.

"Bridesmaid?" This was the **BIG** surprise . . . the special treat Mum and Dad had been whispering about for days.

"Don't look so worried," smiled Uncle Max.

"I've asked my little niece, too," said Bunny. "So there'll be two of you."

"And it's only a short walk up the aisle," grinned Uncle Max.

Of course! Two of us. A short walk. Now everything made sense. . .

Chapter 5

Uncle Max wasn't getting me a puppy. I could see that now.

As the grown-ups hugged one another, I slipped out to the kitchen.

I put away the water bowl I had filled. I folded the sheets of newspaper I had laid down in case my secret-surprise pup wasn't house-trained yet. And I picked up the fluffy towel I had rolled out as a bed.

Uncle Max was getting married! That was the big surprise.

I hardly recognized him any more. It was as if Bunny had waved a secret magic wand and turned him into someone completely different ... someone shiny and **blue** and frilly.

But a flame of hope flickered inside me. This was still Uncle Max we were talking about – cool, crazy SUPER MAX.

I rushed back to the lounge.

"Is the wedding somewhere amazing?" I cried. "Is it on top of a mountain?"

Everyone was gathered around Bunny, peering at a pale blue scrapbook.

"Is it skydiving from a plane? Or underwater in a submarine?" I could see it now! Daredevil Max would leap from a glider. I'd have to skydive too, holding on to Bunny's veil and a bunch of flowers.

Amazing!

Or perhaps I'd follow them down a mountain on a snowboard. My bridesmaid dress wouldn't need to have any frills at all. It probably wouldn't even be a dress. It'd be a special bridesmaid wetsuit with deep-sea-diving oxygen tank. Or flying goggles with a parachute suit and. . .

"Er." Uncle Max looked down at his shiny blue shoes. "Bunny is in charge of most of the wedding arrangements," he said.

"I've chosen WORLD OF WEDDINGS," Bunny grinned.

"Is that on top of a mountain?" I said hopefully.

"No, silly! It's by the big roundabout on the edge of town," laughed Bunny. "I've picked the Dingley Dell wedding theme. They decorate the whole ceiling with gorgeous golden clouds. There are green rubber mats which look exactly like grass.

Plus over two thousand plastic flowers and trees."

"Wow," said Dad. "It sounds ... er ... almost as good as a real field."

"Better," said Bunny. "There's no mud. And they play a recording of real birdsong and a babbling brook."

"Lovely!" said Mum, smiling as hard as she could. "I'm sure it'll be ... wonderful ... and ... er ... very ... clean."

"Exactly," said Bunny. "I've been planning a Dingley Dell wedding for years. You see, my ex-boyfriend, Tarquin, was allergic to pollen. So we could never have got married outside because of his hay fever..."

"But you're not marrying this Tarquin, whoever he is," I blurted out. "Uncle Max doesn't have hay fever. You could marry him in a real field and— *OUCH!*"

Mum poked me in the ribs.

"I'm sure you have wonderful ideas about what everyone is going to wear, Bunny?" she said, smiling harder than ever. "Have you given any thought to Violet's bridesmaid dress?"

"Oh yes! I knew what Vi looked like from the photos Maxi showed me." Bunny held up the shiny blue book.

BUNNY'S BIG WEDDING PLAN

it said in turquoise glitter writing across the front.

"I've chosen a shepherdess theme," she smiled.

Bunny opened the book and we all stared down at a drawing of a bridesmaid with a short brown bob haircut and freckles. I think it was supposed to be me.

HELP!

The girl in the picture was wearing a frilly blue dress with big puffy sleeves and blue lace petticoats. A shiny blue bonnet with shiny blue ribbons perched on her head. She was carrying a shepherdess crook with a big blue bow. It was worse than anything I could have imagined.

HELP! HELP! *HELP!*

"Wow," laughed Tiffany. "I never thought I'd see Violet looking like that."

"I don't think anyone ever thought they'd see

Violet looking like that!" snorted Dad.

"I think it's . . . adorable," said Mum. "She'll look like Little Bo Peep from the nursery rhyme."

"Exactly," I mumbled. "That's the problem."

Mum poked me in the ribs again.

"*OUCH*!" Being a bridesmaid at this wedding was definitely **NOT** going to be fun.

Bunny left me a copy of the bridesmaid picture so that I could look at it whenever I wanted to . . . which was **NEVER**. But I did show it to Nisha when she came round for a sleepover that afternoon.

"Oh Violet." Nisha's big brown eyes twinkled with laughter. "You're going to look so . . . so. . ."

She couldn't seem to find the right word.

"So. . ."

"Ridiculous?" I asked.

"No. . ." I could see the corner of Nisha's mouth moving upwards. "You're going to look so . . . frilly!" she giggled, helplessly.

"Thanks a lot," I groaned. This was not turning into a good weekend. First my dreams of getting a puppy were **TOTALLY** smashed. Now my kindest, loveliest friend had collapsed in fits of laughter at the thought of me in that **Little Bo FREAK** bridesmaid dress.

"It's so unfair," I groaned, throwing a cushion at her. "You looked gorgeous at your uncle's wedding. You got to wear that beautiful yellow sari."

"And you'll look gorgeous too. Really," said Nisha, trying to sound like she meant it.

"Rubbish!" I snatched the picture out of

her hand and stomped out of the house. "There's only one place for this and that's the dustbin."

"Stop!" Nisha grabbed the back of my T-shirt. She tried to pull me back towards her. "Don't throw it away."

"Only because you want to laugh," I said.

As Nisha tugged me in one direction, I grabbed hold of the top of the paper recycling bin and tugged in the other.

CRASH!

The paper bin came toppling down and Nisha and I fell to the ground amongst piles of cardboard and old magazines.

"Look," cooed Nisha. "What a cute kitten."

She was staring down at the crumpled advertisement for PAW THINGS PET RESCUE.

"The sheepdog puppy is adorable, too,"
she said.

But I wasn't looking at the picture. I was
staring at the writing.

I understood what it meant now. PAW THINGS wanted people to go along and help look after the animals.

"But this is brilliant!" I exclaimed, flinging my arms around Nisha's neck. "Why didn't I think of it before?" I flapped the leaflet under her nose. "I am a genius. A TOTAL GENIUS!"

"Have you thought of a plan so you won't have to wear that horrible bridesmaid dress?"

"Better than that," I said, jumping to my feet. "This is the next stage of Operation Get a Dog . . . and this time it DEFINITELY won't fail."

I started to cartwheel down the path but stopped myself mid-spring.

"At least, I think it's quite a good plan," I shrugged casually. I had to stay calm. This was NOT the time to get overexcited. Whatever happened, I didn't want to shrink now.

I stuffed armfuls of cardboard back into the bin. "Let's go inside," I said, holding tight to the PAW THINGS advert. My heart was pounding like a drum.

CHAPTER 6

The *PAW THINGS* leaflet had given me a **BRILLIANT** idea. Uncle Max was too busy getting married to think about getting me a puppy. But it didn't mean I had to give up on a dog altogether.

"Listen, Nish," I said as we flopped down on the sofa. But as soon as I tried to tell her my plan, I could feel excitement jiggling inside me. It was like little bits of bouncy popcorn waiting to explode.

"Are you all right?" said Nish. "Why do you keep pinching your leg like that?"

"Oh . . . er . . . pins and needles," I said.

"Now you're pinching your ear," she said. "You're being really odd today, Violet."

This was hopeless. I have wished a million-zillion times that I could tell Nisha about my shrinking. Imagine the fun we could have. I could ride in her pocket and we could go on mini adventures. She collects china fairy people. I know she'd love to pretend I was a little elf or something. But that's the tricky part about keeping things **TOP SECRET**: you can't tell anyone. Not even your very best friend.

"Hold on a minute," I said, dashing to the kitchen. "I fancy a raw onion. Do you want one?"

"No thank you," Nisha spluttered. "Have you gone mad?"

"They're delicious," I said, plonking myself on

the sofa again. I peeled off the brown skin and took

a big eye-watering bite.

"Just like an apple," I lied, turning away

so she couldn't see my whole face scrunch up.

If I could manage to munch my way through an entire bitter onion, I might be able to tell Nisha my exciting plan without shrinking.

"Stage Two of Operation Get a Dog is incredibly *A WESOME* and incredibly simple," I said, taking another nose-tingling bite. I smoothed out the *PAW THINGS* advertisement on the coffee table. I couldn't actually see it because my eyes were streaming with tears.

"Oh Vi," said Nisha, putting her arms around me. "Are you crying because of the poor stray dogs in the rescue centre?"

"No. It's the onion," I sniffed.

"You really are crazy." Nisha burst into a fit of laughter.

"Maybe you're right," I said, laughing too. "But please, just listen to my plan."

Nisha nodded.

"PAW THINGS needs volunteers to help them," I said. "It'll be jobs like cleaning cages, and walking and feeding the animals. If I go EVERY weekend, I'll get to spend loads of time with the dogs."

"Sounds amazing," agreed Nisha, handing me a tissue to wipe my eyes.

"And ... even more BRILLIANT than that," I said, "Mum and Dad will see how utterly, completely responsible I am. They'll have to let me get a puppy then."

Nisha clapped her hands. "Can I come along, too?"

"Of course you can!" I dropped the onion and spun Nisha around the room, TOTALLY forgetting to keep calm.

"I was super-double-choc-chip-with-extra-sprinkles

hoping you'd come! It's going to be totally brilliant."

"Totally-double-choc-sprinkle brilliant!" agreed Nisha.

"Mum and Dad will be sure to agree if they know you're coming to **PAW THINGS** too," I said as we stopped spinning. "I have no idea why, but they're *FOREVER* saying what a good influence you are."

I looked at Nisha, expecting her to stick her tongue out at me or something, but the smile had vanished from her face.

"I can never have a pet of my own," she sighed. "Because of Rakesh." Her little brother is allergic to animal hair. "But if you get a dog, Violet, it'll be the next best thing to having one of my own."

"Oh, Nish. If I do get one, you can be his

special sleepover owner," I said. "He'll curl up on the end of your bed whenever you come and stay. We can walk him in the park and you can groom him as often as you like."

"Really?" Nisha's face broke into a huge smile.

"Double-choc promise," I said, swallowing the last bite of onion.

I grabbed hold of Nisha's long, neat plaits and tied them under her chin. "Now you look like Little Bo Peep," I grinned.

"Well, at least my breath doesn't STINK of onion," she giggled, holding her nose.

As we ate supper (it was onion soup!) Nisha helped persuade Mum and Dad we should visit PAW THINGS as soon as possible.

"While the idea is fresh in our minds," she

said shyly to them. She sounded all scientific and serious. Like she was talking about an important piece of homework or something. That's one of the reasons Mum and Dad like Nisha so much. She's SUPER clever – top of our class – and her handwriting is even neater than our teacher Miss Penman's!

"Hmm." Mum ladled BIG chunks of onion and sloppy brown water into our bowls. "Helping out at the centre might just stop Violet from thinking about a dog of her own," she said.

That was NOT part of the plan.

"It will show you how responsible I can be," I said, trying to copy Nisha's best-most-sensible-serious face (I think it just looked as if I'd swallowed a chunk of onion the wrong way). "Helping out at the centre is a very important job."

"I'm sure it is," said Dad.

"I can TOTALLY be trusted," I said.

"Some chance!" spluttered Tiffany.

"Oh dear." I patted her HARD on the back. "Don't choke on your onion, Tiff."

"See," I said, looking sweetly at Mum. "Responsible Act Number 1. Saving my sister from choking to death."

Mum raised her eyebrows. "I suppose helping at the centre might make you realize how much work is involved keeping a puppy," she said.

"Sounds like a plan," said Dad. "I could run you up there tomorrow. I want to pop to the electrical shop anyway. I think I've blown a fuse on that toaster."

"Thank you! You won't regret it." I swallowed great gulps of YUCKY onion soup to keep the excitement squished down inside me.

"Operation Get a Dog: Stage Two is under way," I whispered to Nish. Then I leapt up and cleared away the plates – slowly, carefully and very responsibly.

CHAPTER 7

First thing next morning, Dad dropped us at

PAW THINGS PET RESCUE on the outskirts

of Swanchester.

He had to sign a permission form saying we

were allowed to help the staff. This meant we

could feed the animals and take them for walks in

the big orchard behind the kennels.

"See you later," said Dad when he'd signed the

last piece of paper. "Don't get into any mischief.

And DON'T bring home any dogs."

"You'll need to find Yana," smiled a man in a blue vet's coat. "She's in the kennels. A Russian lady. You can't miss her. Through the door at the end."

"Come on, Violet." Nisha skipped ahead and pushed open the door.

"Wait!" I cried.

This was it. The moment I would actually get to see the dogs. I breathed deeply.

"Please don't shrink," I whispered under my breath. If only I had some pepper . . . or an onion. Or a copy of my spellings here. . .

"Hold on." There was a small gift stand beside the reception counter. I spotted a pocket notebook and pencil with *Paw Things Pet Rescue* written across the cover. "Are those for sale?"

Nisha looked at me as if I really was mad now. But through the half-open door, I could hear the sound of barking. Butterflies were swirling in my tummy.

"They cost a pound," said the vet as I took a notebook and dropped my pocket money into the donation tin.

"Times tables," I explained, scribbling madly.

My hand was shaking as I gripped the little pencil and wrote:

$7 \times 7 = 49$

$9 \times 7 =$

"Why are you doing that now?" hissed Nisha. "I thought you wanted to see the dogs?"

The vet was drumming his fingers impatiently on the counter.

"Come on," begged Nisha. "Let's go!"

"I'm hopeless at my seven times table," I said. "It's my worst one. Miss Penman is so strict if we don't know all the way up to our twelves."

"Really strict," agreed Nisha as I scribbled another sum.

$7 \times 4 = ?$

What does *seven times four equal?* I screwed up my eyebrows trying to concentrate. This was perfect. Times tables were nearly as good as spellings for making sure I didn't get too excited.

If I shrank to the size of the pocket pencil I was writing with, there was NO WAY anybody would ever let me look after a dog. Not even the smallest chihuahua in the world.

"Got it . . . twenty-eight." I smiled at the vet.

"You seem a little reluctant to go through to the kennel," he said. "If you're scared of dogs, you can always help with the kittens instead."

"Scared? No!" I gasped. "I love dogs! **BIG**
ones, small ones, SPOTTY ones..."

"We double-choc-sprinkle love them," agreed
Nisha, backing me up.

"We can't wait to get in there," I said. "Come
on!" I pushed Nisha through the door to the kennels.

"Wow!" The sound of barking was deafening.

I caught glimpse of a spotty Dalmatian. My
heart gave a **GIANT** leap.

And my toes began to tingle...

Oh no! Had all those times tables been for
nothing?

Nisha was skipping along ahead of me.

"Look," she said, pointing to the nearest cage,
where the Dalmatian was sleeping with its head on
its paws.

WHOOSH!

I shrank faster than I've ever shrunk before –
like a yo-yo shooting down a string.

"Whoa!" I gasped. My head was spinning. I dived
sideways as the notebook clattered to the ground
beside me. The pocket pencil followed, crashing
past me like a falling tree. "Yikes!"

Nisha spun round.

"Violet?" She looked round helplessly.
"Violet? Where are you?"

I couldn't let her
see me. Not now.

I dived under the
notebook, pulling it
over my head like
a tiny tent.

"Hello?" A Russian-sounding voice called from inside the cage next to the Dalmatian. "It is the girls, yes?"

I peeped out through the doorway of my notebook tent.

"I am so glad you are here to help me," said the voice. "I am Yana."

Cool! A young woman with a pierced nose and tall spikes of bright green hair poked her head out of the cage.

"Er . . . h-hello!" Nisha took a tiny step back. The vet had said that Yana would be easy to find. He never mentioned that her hair was the shape and colour of a prickly cactus.

WICKED! I thought. If only Mum would let me do that to mine.

"I was expecting two children?" Yana glanced

around. "Two girls. No?" Her head disappeared inside the cage again.

"No . . . I mean, yes," spluttered Nisha. "I . . . er. . . There are two of us. I mean, there were."

Poor Nish. She hates getting in a muddle. But of course she had no idea where I had gone.

"My friend Violet was worried about her times tables," she explained. "So perhaps she. . . Oh?" Nisha spotted my notebook on the floor.

Hide! I thought. But it was too late. Nisha scooped up the pad with one hand. I was left crouching on the ground as if a GIANT whirlwind

had blown my tent away.

CHAPTER 8

Normally I am exactly the same height as Nisha, but now she towered HIGH above me.

"Violet?" Her hands flew to her mouth.

All the colour drained from her face.

"Is that you?" she gasped, bending down.

"Shhh." I pressed a tiny finger to my lips, hoping she'd understand and keep quiet.

"Yes, Nish. It's me," I said. There was nothing else for it. She had seen me now. There was nowhere I could hide.

"**AAhhhhhhhh!** What's happened to you?" Nisha screamed so loud the Dalmatian started to howl.

"**AROOOOOOO!**"

I dived behind a sack of dog biscuits and covered my tiny ears. It did no good. All the other dogs started too.

"**AROOOOOOO!**"
"**AROOOOOOO!**"

"**AROOOOOOO!**"

Something really big had joined in.

With all the howling and Nisha's screaming, I thought my little eardrums would burst.

"What is the matter?" cried Yana, dashing out of the cage to see what was going on.

"My friend!" screamed Nisha. "My friend has shrun—"

I peeped out from behind the dog biscuits and shook my head.

"Shhh!" I put my miniature finger to my lips again.

"Don't say anything," I begged as the sound of howling drowned my small voice. "PLEASE!"

It was bad enough that Nisha had seen me, but if I was spotted by a total stranger, everyone would know my shrinking secret.

"What is wrong?" asked Yana kindly. "Your friend is what?"

I poked my head quickly round the edge of the dog biscuits. I saw Yana lay her hand on Nisha's shoulder.

"She's. . ." Nisha glanced towards the bag, her

dark eyes as **HUGE** as saucers. "She's. . ."

I took another tiny step forward. I was still hidden in the shadows but I tried to beam up good thoughts. Nisha and I once told our arch enemy, Ratty-Riley, that we could read each other's minds. Nish got a football and covered it with one of her mum's scarves to pretend it was a crystal ball. If only she really could read my mind. This would be the moment for it to work.

"She's . . . she's gone to the toilet," said Nisha, at last.

"Yes! THANK YOU, NISH!" I knew she wouldn't let me down. She couldn't really read my mind, of course. But that's the good thing about being best friends – we always know what the other one wants.

I crept back behind the dog biscuits. As I

peered out of the shadows I could see that Nisha's legs were shaking. She was chewing her bottom lip. I wished I could just run over to her and tell her everything would be OK. She'd screamed so loud when she saw that I was tiny. Perhaps she wouldn't even want to be my friend any more? The thought jolted me like an electric shock. What if she didn't want me to hide in her pocket and go for adventures? What if she was too scared to come near me ever again?

"Your friend has gone to the toilet?" Yana was laughing. "Is that all?" She scratched between the spikes of her green hair and shrugged. "Then why were you shouting? You were scaring the dogs." For the first time, she sounded stern.

"I'm so sorry." A blush spread across Nisha's dark skin. Even from behind the sack of biscuits,

I could see her eyes filling up with tears. She hates being told off.

I had to do something to help her explain why she had screamed.

"Eeeek! Eeeek! Eeeek!" I squeaked as LOUD as I could, hoping Nisha would pick up the clue.

"Eeeek!" I scuttled away, slipping behind a roll of hosepipe.

"I screamed because ... because I thought I saw a mouse," said Nisha, taking the hint. "I really didn't mean to scare the dogs."

"A mouse?" Yana smiled, sounding friendly again. "They make me jump, too. They come sometimes looking for crumbs of food. Now, I will fetch a cat," she said.

"A cat?" gasped Nisha. She glanced helplessly towards the roll of hose.

"A big stray tomcat," said Yana. "He will catch the mouse. *POW!*" She clapped her hands. "Just like that."

"Oh dear," quivered Nisha.

My knees felt weak. Suddenly, pretending to be a mouse didn't seem like such a totally brilliant idea.

CHAPTER 9

"Please, Yana. Don't bring a cat into the kennels," begged Nisha, edging towards the roll of hosepipe, where I was crouched like a tiny terrified mouse.

"No cat?" said Yana, stopping by the door. "Why? Are you allergic?"

"Well . . . no," struggled Nisha. "But wouldn't a cat be frightened in here?" Some of the dogs were still barking and howling from when Nisha had screamed.

BRILLIANT! Quick thinking, Nish! I really

did not want to be chased by a **BIG** HUNGRY kitty.

"You are right," nodded Yana. "I will fetch a cat later when the dogs have calmed down."

"Great," breathed Nisha.

"Phew!" I leant back against the hosepipe with a sigh of relief. Being eaten alive was definitely NOT on my list of Top Ten Things To Do Today.

"Come on, Nisha. I'll show you the special dog you are going to help with. Your friend can catch up," said Yana, hurrying round the corner.

"Just coming," said Nisha. But she bent down next to the roll of hosepipe and pretended to tie her shoelace.

"Violet?" she whispered. Everything was going to be all right. I could see it in Nisha's eyes at once. She wasn't scared any more and she wasn't angry I'd got her into trouble. In fact, from the way she was grinning, I think she wanted to pop me in her pocket and add me to the china fairy collection on her window sill at home.

Her eyes sparkled as she held out her hand towards me.

"Thank you!" I scrambled out of the hosepipe and jumped into her palm.

"I'm sorry if I gave you a fright," I said. She held me close to her ear so she could hear my tiny voice.

"This is like something from a storybook," she whispered. "Like *Thumbelina*, or *The Borrowers*, or—"

"Nish," I hissed. "It's secret. I mustn't be seen by anybody else. I'll explain everything later, I promise."

"Right! Of course," she said, closing her hand gently around me.

Nisha slipped me into her cardigan pocket and I peered out over the top as we hurried round the corner.

"Come quietly, Nisha," said Yana, pointing to a tall cage at the end of the row.

Nish crept forward.

Pressed against the bars was a MASSIVE black dog. I could have ridden on his back if I had been **FULL SIZE**. As it was, his sharp front teeth looked longer than I was now. Each paw was the size of a dinner plate, with claws like scissor blades poking out.

"This is Tiny," grinned Yana.

"Tiny?" Nisha gasped.

Whoever named him must have had a sense of humour – either that, or he'd grown **A LOT** since he was a puppy.

"**GRRRRRRR!**"

Tiny sprung at the bars of the cage. He was taller than Yana as he leapt up on his hind legs and snarled at Nisha.

Yikes! *Not exactly a lapdog*, I thought, clinging to the edge of Nisha's pocket as she jumped back.

"Sorry! He is not very friendly," said Yana.

Not very friendly? Tiny looked like he wanted to eat Nisha alive. If he knew I was in her pocket he'd snap me in half like a dog biscuit and gobble me up with one CHOMP of his TERRIBLE JAWS. Surely this wasn't the dog we were supposed to look after?

"His owners could not afford to feed him," said Yana. "He has only been at PAW THINGS for two weeks. He will settle down soon and become our friend."

"I hope so," said Nisha. "He's very . . ."

Fierce? I thought.

". . . dribbly!" said Nisha as pools of sticky doggy drool dripped over Tiny's ENORMOUS gums and splashed on to the tiled floor beneath him.

"WOOF!" Tiny leapt forward to snarl at Nisha again.

A glob of drool as big as an egg yolk flew through the air.

"Eww!" shrieked Nisha. She dived sideways as the giant spitball missed her elbow by a millimetre. I ducked down inside her pocket. But I was too late. The glob of drool landed *SPLAT* on my head and EXPLODED on my hair like a gooey water bomb.

"Agh!" I shuddered as warm slime dribbled down the back of my neck. It made a deep, sticky pool in the bottom of Nisha's pocket.

Thank goodness I'm wearing wellies, I thought.

But Tiny was dangerous! Even if he didn't get to chomp me to death, I might drown in a pool of his doggy drool.

"So, Nisha?" said Yana, brightly. "You want to walk a dog. Yes?"

"You mean this dog?" gulped Nisha, staring at Tiny with her mouth wide open.

"No!" Yana laughed. "I just wanted to show you Tiny. But I'll find something a bit smaller for you and your friend. Come on."

She set off along the row of cages.

"Phew!" Peeping out of Nisha's soggy pocket, I breathed **GIANT** sigh of relief. While I was shorter than a chihuahua's tail, a nice small dog was definitely a good idea.

Nisha must have felt the same because, as we hurried along, she slipped her hand in her pocket.

I think she was trying to tell me that everything was OK.

"GROSS!" she yelped as she plunged her fingers straight into the sticky pool of drool.

"Oh dear," I giggled as she waved her gooey hand in the air. Yana had turned the corner ahead of us now. But the smile froze on my face as I felt a sudden jolt in my stomach and. . .

WHOOSH!

There I was. Back to FULL SIZE! I was lying in a heap on the floor with Nisha squashed underneath me.

"Sorry," I whispered as Nish stared up at me, totally dazed. "Shrinking and growing always happens SUPER fast. I never know how long it's going to last or when I'm going to grow back."

Nisha put her fingers through the hole in her

cardigan pocket where I had burst out of it like a human cannonball.

"Hello there..." Yana's head appeared as she came back round the corner.

I was sure she hadn't actually seen me grow, but she was staring at us lying in a heap on the floor.

"I – er – just came from the toilet," I said, struggling to my feet.

Nisha jumped up too and flung her arms around my neck. "Violet! I'm so glad you're..."

"...here," I said quickly. "Yes. So am I."

Yana opened her mouth and closed it again.

"You girls are a little bit crazy, I think?!"

"A *little, tiny* bit," I said. Nisha giggled.

Yana smiled at me.

"But it's nice to meet you, Violet," she said. "You have such a pretty name. In Russia we would say Violetta, I think."

"Then you can call me that," I said. I liked the way it sounded in her strong accent. Now I was tall enough to look at her properly, I could see that as well as having super-cool green hair, Yana was really pretty and young. She had sparkly hazel eyes and pale white skin.

"I'm sorry I was . . . late," I said. "But I'm here now and ready to work really hard."

"Good," said Yana. "Then follow me. I will show you the dog you will look after. He is very special, I think."

CHAPTER 10

As Yana led us down a row of dog kennels, I squeezed Nisha's hand and did a little skip of joy. I realized how long I had wanted to tell her about my shrinking and how WONDERFUL it felt to share the secret at last. I could see she was BURSTING with questions ... but that would have to wait until we were alone.

"Look!" I cried, pointing all around us. Now I was back to full size, I could see the dogs properly for the first time.

I peered into each cage as we passed. There was a mother with her pups in the first. A yappy brown mongrel with three legs in another. Then five Staffordshire bull terriers all in a row and an old black Labrador with a grey speckled nose.

"Isn't he gorgeous?" I said.

Just ahead of us, Yana stopped. She was standing outside the very last cage in the line. "You can help with all the dogs," she explained. "But I thought it would be fun if you pretend this small chap was your very own."

My heart was pounding again. I pinched myself – hard! A **SPECIAL DOG**, just for us! But when I stepped forward, I couldn't see anything in the cage at all.

"It's empty," I said, disappointment washing over me. Perhaps someone else was looking after him already.

"I can't see anything," Nisha agreed.

"Look again." Yana slid open the bolt.

"Oh!" I cried as something in the basket stirred.

There was a snuffling sound like a piglet and a tiny black nose poked out from under the blanket.

"Ah!" sighed Nisha.

The smallest, **STRANGEST**, CUTEST dog I have ever seen rolled out on to the floor. He stretched and yawned, opening his little

mouth as wide as a sleepy tiger. His podgy belly
hung so low, it was almost scraping along the
ground as he padded across the floor towards us.
He was covered in tufts of WILD, grizzly
brown hair like a tiny baby bear. One ear poked up.
The other looked as if it had been hurt in a fight.
It was torn and ragged like a scrap of old paper.
He had the deepest, darkest
eyes imaginable.

94

"We think he is a little mixed up," said Yana. "A bit of this breed. A bit of that. Perhaps part chug?"

"Chug?" asked Nisha. "What's that?"

"Half chihuahua, half pug," I said, proudly. I had read about them in my **Bumper Book Of Dogs**.

Yana smiled. "I see you know lot about dogs, Violetta. The chihuahua explains why this little fellow is so small..."

"And the pug explains his turned-up nose," I grinned.

"But why is he so long?" asked Nisha as the tiny dog stretched.

"We think there is a bit of wire-haired dachshund in there too," said Yana. "You know, like a hairy sausage dog. That explains his long body and thick coat."

"He's GORGEOUS!" I said, bending down so he could sniff my hand. He snuffled sleepily at the edge of my sleeve and a SHIVER of joy ran through me.

"What's his name?" I asked, pinching the side of my leg.

"We don't know his real name," said Yana. "An old lady found him in a dustbin and brought him to PAW THINGS. He is still young, about two years old. But he had been very badly treated."

"How horrible," I shuddered.

"I call him Chip," said Yana. "Short for Chipolata." She frowned. "Is that how you say it in English? You know, like the little sausages you get on sticks at parties."

"That's the perfect name," I grinned as he

nuzzled me again. "Hello, Chip." I scratched between his shaggy ears. "He's ADORABLE! And look how quiet he is, and so well behaved. Just think! We could have had Tiny instead."

"Oh, Chip is not quiet – just sleepy," grinned Yana. She handed us a little red lead and collar. "Now he is awake, you will see. . ."

"What do you mean?" I said, as Chip shook himself. He rolled on to his back as if he was waiting for his belly to be tickled.

"You will find out," smiled Yana. She pointed through a glass door towards a big sloping field scattered with trees. "We walk the dogs out there in the orchard. If there is any trouble, I will come."

"What sort of trouble could there be?" said Nisha. "There are two of us and he is such a tiny dog."

"Ah, but small dogs make big trouble," warned Yana. And with that she was gone.

As we walked down the path through the **grassy** orchard, Nisha grabbed my sleeve.

"Tell me everything about shrinking," she begged.

"Later," I promised. "Just as soon as we get home. Let's just enjoy being with Chip for now." He trotted along beside us in amongst the apple trees.

"I think he wants to be our friend," Nisha grinned.

He kept glancing up to check we were still there.

"I know how he feels," I laughed. "It's not easy being small." Chip was shorter than the top of my wellington boots. "He's worried he'll be left behind. Or worse, that someone might tread on him. Isn't that right, boy?"

Chip wagged his tail as if to agree.

Every once in a while, he stopped and yawned. I had to give a gentle tug on his lead to make him keep up.

"I don't know what Yana was worried about," said Nisha. "He seems like such a good little dog."

But just at that moment, a squirrel dashed across our path.

"RUFF!" Chip dived forward, and now it was me who felt a tug on the lead.

"Steady!" I cried, trying to haul him backwards as he strained against me. He might have been small but he was chubby too, and super strong. Nisha grabbed hold of the lead as well.

"**RUFF!**" Chip barked again, yapping at the squirrel as it shot up the nearest apple tree.

"Stay, boy!" I said. Chip would never be able get away now. Not with both of us holding the lead.

He flopped down on to his belly and looked up at us sadly, his big dark eyes pleading, as if to say:

Ooh, let me get that squirrel. Let me get him! Please! Please! Please!

"We're not allowed to let you off," I said. "You can't get round us that easily." But as I turned and took a step forward, I felt the lead go limp in my hand.

Chip had wriggled free. There was nothing on the end of lead now but an empty collar.

"RUFF! RUFF! RUFF!" Chip sped off across the orchard like a firework on Bonfire Night.

"Chip!" I bellowed. "You come back here."

"Oh dear," said Nisha as we charged after him.

We ran helter-skelter down the field, but Chip had disappeared in the long grass.

Nisha stopped to clutch her side. "He's vanished," she panted.

"He's got to be here somewhere." I said, looking around desperately. "We can't tell Yana we've lost him. Not yet! The whole point of coming to PAW THINGS was to show Mum and Dad how responsible I could be."

"And Yana already thinks we're crazy," groaned Nisha.

"Chip!" I cried at the top of my voice. "Chip! Where are you?"

CHAPTER 11

Five minutes passed and there was still no sign of Chip.

I looped the empty lead around my shoulders.

"We better go back," said Nisha. "If we tell Yana what's happened, perhaps she can help find him."

I knew Nisha was right.

"Let's just go round once more," I begged. "Perhaps he's right down the bottom in those bushes."

There were only about five or six apple trees

spread out across the orchard – it was more like a big field, really, although it was surrounded by a high brick wall. The grass was criss-crossed with stony paths that sloped downhill towards a scruffy tangle of brambles and tall weeds. I was sure that was where Chip would be.

"I don't know," said Nisha. "I think we ought to—"

"Wait," I held up my hand. "What's that?"

"RUFF! RUFF! RUFF!"

"Chip!" Already I'd recognize that strange little bark anywhere. "See – he's in the bushes!" I cried as a squirrel shot out of the undergrowth and flew up the nearest tree.

A moment later Chip dashed after it. He was running so fast it looked as if he had a hundred tiny legs instead of four.

"You are the funniest dog I've ever seen," I laughed, dashing forward with my arms spread wide. "Now sit, boy! Sit!"

I leapt in front of him. But Chip shot straight through my legs, still barking at the squirrel.

"Catch him, Nisha!" I cried.

Nisha dived. She nearly caught him round the tummy but Chip swerved sideways.

The squirrel was long gone. But Chip wanted

to play with us instead. Every time we leapt forward, he dived sideways, dodging behind nearby apple trees . . . always just out of reach.

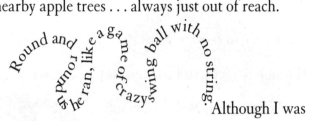 Round and round he ran, like a game of crazy swingball with no string. Although I was scared we might never catch him, it was brilliant fun.

"This is a great game," I laughed.

The faster we ran, the more Chip yapped.

"RUFF! RUFF! RUFF!"

"This dog is a tiny terror," exclaimed Nisha, tears of laughter streaming down her face.

"A total tearaway!" I agreed as I slipped down the slope on my bum. "Yana did try to warn us."

I collapsed in an exhausted heap on the grass.

"Oh, Chip," I sighed. "What are we going to do with you?"

OOMPH! He leapt into my open arms.

"Got you!" I hugged him tight.

"Look how he's wagging his tail," smiled Nisha.

I flopped on to my back and Chip lay panting with his shaggy head resting on my chest.

"Are you exhausted from being soooOOOO **NAUGHTY**?" I said.

Chip wagged his tail again.

"He really likes you, Violet," said Nisha. "I can tell."

"Do you think so?" I grinned. But I knew it was true. As Chip looked at me with his big, black, watery eyes, I felt a sharp tingling in my toes.

"Don't look at me like that," I warned Chip. But it was too late – the tingling had spread to my fingertips already.

"Nish!" I squeaked. "Get Chip off me. I think I'm going to shr..."

But it was too late. I had already shrunk. My voice was tiny and I was buried underneath Chip's podgy tummy – squashed like a lost key under a sofa cushion.

"Let me out!" I squealed. I wriggled and squiggled and squirmed.

It must have tickled because Chip leapt up and scratched his tummy wildly with his back leg.

"Careful!" cried Nisha.

"I'm not a flea, you know, Chip," I said, leaping out of the way.

Chip stopped scratching and stared down at me. He wrinkled his nose and sniffed my hair.

"Stop! Now you're tickling me," I squealed as Chip tried to push me over with his nose. He opened his mouth. His tongue was hanging down like a piece of wet cloth.

"Yuck!" I leapt backwards as a splash of drool hit the ground. I'd only just recovered from being dribbled on by Tiny.

"Look out!" shouted Nisha. "He's going to lick you. He thinks you're a lolly."

But Chip didn't lick me. Instead he lifted me in

his jaws . . . and **ran off at top speed**. My head was hanging out of one side of his mouth and my feet out of the other, like a sausage in a hot-dog bun.

"Stop!" cried Nisha.

"Bad boy!" I squealed. I knew Chip wasn't going to eat me – his grip was far too gentle for that – it was more as if I were his favourite toy. I was stuck between his squishy gums while he dribbled all over me like I was a soggy chew bone.

"Ew!" I was really going to need to have a good bath tonight.

Chip seemed to think this was all just another game.

When Nisha dived left, he dived right. If she crawled, he bounced. If she ran, he ZOOOOOOOOMED!

"PUT HER DOWN!" ordered Nisha.

"RUFF!" barked Chip. I almost fell out of his mouth but he closed his jaws again.

I'm having far too much fun, he seemed to

laugh to himself. *I am never, never, never going to put her down.*

Why hadn't I slipped his lead and collar back on when I had the chance?

He still held me firmly, but he never clamped his teeth tight shut. Nisha didn't know this, of course. She must have thought I was being chewed alive.

"DROP!" she begged as Chip danced from side to side in front of her.

Suddenly, a loud sharp shrill whistle blew: **VREEEEEEEEEEEEEEW!**

Chip stopped in his tracks and stared towards the kennels. Yana was standing in the doorway.

From inside Chip's jaws I felt him slump. He knew he was being naughty. It reminded me of the saggy feeling I get in my shoulders when Miss Penman spots me doing cartwheels in the corridor at school.

"Where is Violetta?" Yana called. "Are you having a problem, Nisha?"

"Yes! Chip wriggled out of his collar." Nisha held up the empty lead. "I can't catch him. Now he's got Vi—"

"NO!" I called out desperately, hoping that Nisha could hear me. Yana was still too far away for my tiny voice to carry. "CHIP ISN'T GOING TO HURT ME! I'M FINE!"

"Come on, Trouble," said Yana, jogging down the path. "Think you could escape, did you?" In one swift movement she bent down and scooped Chip up.

"Back to the kennel with you," she said, clutching him under her arm like a little fat handbag. She never noticed me, of course, buried under the fuzzy whiskers around his mouth.

Poor Nisha jogged alongside, looking worried and chewing her nails.

If only I could tell her I had a plan.

Chip was sure to drop me once he was back in his cage. Then I could slip through the bars and Nish could look after me until I grew back to full size.

One small problem! All that running had made Chip thirsty. . .

As soon as Yana put him in his cage, he made a dash for his water bowl.

"AHHHHHHHHH!"

The second his jaws were open, I p l
u
n
g
e
d

towards the water.

"Geronimo!" With a super-quick, super-cool move Uncle Max had taught me on the trampoline, I spun myself over in a backflip.

But. . .

SPLOSH!

Without the springy trampoline, I wasn't fast enough. I sat in the water bowl right up to my neck as if I were taking a very deep, very COLD bath.

I squelched to the side, sat on the edge of the bowl and emptied my tiny soggy wellies.

"Where has Violetta gone?" said Yana, taking the lead and collar from Nisha. She fastened the bolt and locked Chip's door. "Her father has come to collect you both. It is time to go home."

"Erm . . . she's in the toilet again," said Nisha, helplessly glancing towards me as I ducked down, dripping wet, behind Chip's water bowl. "Perhaps she wanted to have a wash."

It was more than a wash! I was soaked to the skin. I was about to peep out and do a funny dance in my wellies just to show Nisha that I was OK. But as I looked at the front of the cage, my heart sank.

There was no way out of here.

Unlike the bars in Tiny's kennel, which were set wide apart, Chip's cage was covered with tight wire mesh.

The holes in the wire were minute. Each one was no bigger than the end of a felt-tip pen lid. Even though I was tiny, there was no way I could squeeze through.

Dad was waiting to take me home. But I was **locked** in the cage . . . stuck on the wrong side of the wire like a rabbit in a hutch.

CHAPTER 12

Still dripping wet, I crouched behind Chip's water bowl and stared helplessly up through the wire.

Nisha kept glancing in my direction. The whole idea of shrinking was so new to her, I hoped she wouldn't panic and say anything to give me away.

Yana patted her on the back.

"Thank you for help," she said. "You and Violetta are welcome to come to **PAW THINGS** again."

"Really?" Nisha sounded as if she couldn't believe it.

"Of course! It is not so bad you let Chip go," smiled Yana. "He is a rascal. Yes?"

"Yes," agreed Nisha. Chip **wagged** his whole body from side to side, squirming with excitement because he knew they were talking about him. He nearly knocked me over with his tail, which was spinning around like a propeller blade in front of my nose. I was so small, I think he had forgotten I was there.

"You and Violetta can enter Chip in the dog show next month if you like," said Yana.

A dog show? I stood up on tiptoes. Had Yana really said we could enter Chip? That would be AMAZING.

"PAW THINGS have a dog show every year

to raise money," Yana explained. "It is a very big event with lots of prizes. A real chance for dogs and humans to show off." Yana laughed.

"Oh. . ." said Nisha, sounding uncertain. But I peered round the side of the water bowl and gave her a mini thumbs up.

This was brilliant! A dog show would be the PERFECT chance to show Mum and Dad how well I could handle a dog. OK, Chip and I might need a bit more practice. But we could enter something easy like Dog With the Waggiest Tail . . . or The Shortest Legs contest.

"We could both win that," I giggled to myself as Chip flopped down on the floor and closed his eyes for a nap.

"Violetta's father is waiting," Yana was saying to Nisha. "You better tell him she is on her way."

"Er ... right..." Nisha looked helplessly towards the water bowl.

"Go," I mouthed, pointing in that direction with my tiny finger. Yana glanced over to see what Nisha was staring at and I dived behind the water bowl, out of sight.

I was sure I could find a way to escape from the cage once Yana was gone, but I needed Nisha to go to Dad and make up a good excuse about why I was late. Otherwise he'd just think I was being **IRRESPONSIBLE**, keeping him waiting.

"Perhaps Violetta has a poorly tummy?" I heard Yana say as she led Nisha back towards the reception. "She is spending so much time in the toilet."

"Yes . . . that must be it," agreed Nisha.

I hoped she would tell Dad the same thing. It

would be a good way to explain where I had gone and why I was taking so long.

Now all I had to do was find a way to escape from Chip's kennel. Then, with a little bit of luck, I'd grow back to full size and be able to catch up with Nisha *SUPER-QUICK*.

"But getting out of here won't be easy," I said, smiling at Chip.

I stepped back to get a better view of the cage.

"Aha!" The wire didn't actually reach all the way to the roof. There was a small gap between the top of the cage and the ceiling – about as tall as a box of cereal. I could just about **SQUEEZE** through even if I was full size, but it would be **EASY** while I was mini. The climb to reach it might take a while ... but I am pretty quick. I practise climbing all the time in the adventure playground at King's Park.

"Bye, Chip," I said, stretching up to scratch behind his ear. He nuzzled me happily. I don't think he really minded that I was miniature. Dogs know people mostly by their smell. I suppose that would be the same whether I was as tall as a girl or as small as a pine cone.

"See you soon." I leapt up on the wire and began the steep climb. If only there was some way I could catch up with Nisha. I could hide under her collar or swing on her plaits, whispering excuses so she could tell Dad why I was late. I knew he'd want to know where I had been.

"Oh, just hanging around," I giggled to myself as I dangled from the wire by one arm.

Far below, I could see Chip staring up at me like a small, short-legged mountain goat.

"RIFF! RIFF!" he barked, his strange little yap now sounding more like a whine.

Get down! Get down! he seemed to say.

"Don't worry, Chip. I'm having FUN," I replied.

It's one of the reasons I love shrinking . . . I get to do THRILLING, DAREDEVIL SUPER-STUNTS like this. The sorts of things grown-ups never let you do even when you're full size.

"RIFF!" whimpered Chip again.

"Don't you want me to go?" I said, and a warm smile spread across my tiny face.

Chip loves me, I thought.

"Don't worry. I'll come again soon. I promise," I said.

I was at the top of the cage already. All I had to do was swing my feet over and climb down the other side. It should be much quicker than it had been scrambling up.

"YIKES!" I tried not to look down as I wriggled my body over the edge of the wire.

"Whoops!" As I swung my leg over to the other side, one of my tiny wellies slipped off the end of my foot.

D
o
w
n
it fell, plunging to the ground. It bounced like a rubber ball when it hit the floor, disappearing down the side of a drain.

"Oh dear, Chip," I laughed, shouting down to him and trying not to lean too far over the edge.

"I hope I can find that when I..."

"Hello?" A voice interrupted me. The patter of footsteps came closer.

"Hello?" called the voice again. "Is anybody there?"

There was something familiar about that voice. Something squeaky and whiny and...

"Ratty-Riley," I gasped at the exact same moment that my arch enemy, Riley Paterson, came round the corner.

What is he doing here? I thought.

"**GRUFF!**" Chip leapt at the wire and barked. It seemed he didn't like the look of Ratty-Riley either.

"Help!" Riley jumped in the air. "Horrid little mutt. You frightened me," he said.

"**GRUFF! GRUFF! GRUFF!**" Chip barked louder than ever.

I stayed as still as I could. I had no idea why Riley was here. I couldn't let him see me. But as he turned his back, I felt a sudden lurch in my stomach and. . .

POP!

There I was, back to FULL SIZE, clinging to the very top of the wire.

Why do I always have to grow back at the worst possible moment? I wondered. I know now that I shrink whenever I am overexcited. But growing back just seems to happen all of a sudden – totally by surprise.

"Ahhhh!" Riley spun round. This time he jumped higher than a kangaroo. "Violet Potts! What. . .? Why. . .? How did you get there?"

He stood there opening and closing his mouth like a goldfish.

I wish I could have thought of something clever to say. But the wire was swaying dangerously under my FULL weight. All I could do was scream:

"HELP!"

CHAPTER 13

As soon as Ratty-Riley had got over the shock of seeing me, he started to snigger.

"Grab a ladder," I cried as I swung helplessly from the wire. Even though I was full size now, the drop to the floor was still pretty big.

"A ladder?" Riley was either more stupid than I thought or he was pretending not to understand me.

I nodded my head towards the door to the orchard. I'd seen a ladder out there leaning against one of the trees.

"Hmm. A ladder?" said Riley. Now I knew he was pretending.

"Come on, Riley!" I shouted as the wire buckled again. Couldn't he see it was serious? If I fell from here I might break my leg . . . or at least twist my ankle.

"Why should I?" he grinned.

I knew there was no point in begging or asking him nicely. Ratty-Riley doesn't work that way.

"Because if you help me, I'll buy you a **TOFFAMEL** bar," I said, naming my favourite crispy chocolate.

"Two **TOFFAMELS** and I might think about it," said Riley.

"Fine! **JUST GET THE LADDER!**"

I screamed as my foot slipped – it was the one with just a sock, where I'd lost my tiny welly.

I was left dangling by one arm.

Even Riley looked worried, as he dashed for the ladder pretty quick.

"I'm telling on you," he whined as I reached the ground safely at last. "I bet you weren't supposed to be up there."

"I got locked in," I said, truthfully. "Me and

Nisha are helping out here." I pointed proudly at Chip. "That's our special dog!"

"That thing?" Riley clutched his stomach and laughed. "Is it even a dog? I thought it was a guinea pig."

Chip growled as if to show what a **BIG**, FIERCE dog he really was. The trouble is, he was wagging his tail at the same time.

"Just you wait, Riley," I said. "There's going to be a dog show and Chip's going to get first prize."

"Ha!" Riley laughed harder than ever. "That's why I'm here. I want to pick up an entry form for the *Dog and Child Agility Trial*. My dad reckons I'm sure to win."

"Agility?" I snorted. "Like jumping over fences and crawling through hoops?"

I'd beaten Riley at every race on Sports Day

last year – including the egg and spoon and the obstacle race.

"Yeah," sneered Riley. "Don't tell me you're going to enter that thing in the Agility Trial, too?"

I turned to look at Chip. How dare Riley insult him. He wagged his tail and stared up at me, his head cocked to one side.

"Of course I am going to enter him," I said. "And I bet you ... **FIVE** bars of **TOFFAMEL** we can win."

Agility? What was I thinking? The minute the words were out of my mouth I wished I could stuff them back in.

Five bars of **TOFFAMEL**? It was a crazy bet. Chip's legs were so short he had trouble stepping over a hosepipe, never mind leaping through a hoop. His back was so long that his head always seemed to be doing something quite different from his tail. His little belly was so tubby it practically scraped along the ground. He'd never be able to leap over a doggy-show jump . . . even if I did train him to catch a ball, fetch and sit. At the moment, I couldn't even get him to come back when I called.

Why hadn't I said we'd enter The Dog With the Waggiest Tail like I had planned? Anything other than AGILITY.

"Let's make it TEN bars of TOFFAMEL," said Riley, striding away.

"Ten? No way!" I hopped after him on one foot. There was still no sign of my lost welly anywhere. It must have slipped away down the drain.

"Ten bars," said Riley. "That's the bet. Unless you're scared that little guinea pig can't win." He

pointed at Chip, who was jumping up and down
in his cage.

"He's not a guinea pig," I said. "He's a wire-
haired sausage dog cross chug – a bit of this, a bit
of that. But he can beat you **ANYTIME**."

"Then it's a bet," called Riley as he scuttled off
towards reception. "I hope there's someone there

so I can pick up an entry form now. I want to enter me and Speedy right away."

"Speedy?" I gulped. That really didn't sound good. Surely Riley was making that name up.

"Er . . . what sort of dog is Speedy?" I called after him.

"You'll see." Riley flashed me his rattiest, toothiest, meanest grin. Then the door banged shut and he was gone.

Before I went to bed that night, Mum pushed a glass of thick purple prune juice across the kitchen table.

"Nisha told Dad you were in the toilet when you kept him waiting this afternoon. If you were in there that long, you must be having . . . *problems going*." Mum whispered this last bit. She always does that when she has to mention embarrassing things to do with bodies or going to the loo. "Prune juice is marvellous for *that sort of thing*."

YUCK!

"Actually I wasn't in the toilet," I said. "I was . . . I was talking to Riley Paterson."

"I don't believe that for a moment," laughed Mum. "You never talk to Riley Paterson."

"But it's true," I promised. "I was climbing out of Chip's cage and—"

"Just drink the prune juice, Violet," sighed Mum. "I suppose you'll tell me it was Riley's fault you lost your wellington boot, too?"

"No," I said, truthfully – though I'd have loved to blame Ratty-Riley if I could. "I am really sorry about that . . . although they *were* getting a bit small for me." I thought about how tiny the little lost wellington must be, floating in a drain somewhere. The other one had grown back to full size when I did. Anything I'm wearing always shrinks and grows along with me. But as I had dropped the boot while I was mini, I supposed it would stay that size for ever. If anyone found it, they'd think it belonged to a doll . . . or Thumbelina.

The thought made me smile.

"I don't know why you're looking so happy," said Mum. "You can buy a new pair of wellies out of your pocket money. I thought you were trying to show me how responsible you can be?"

"I am DEFINITELY responsible," I said. "Look!" I drank down the thick, LUMPY prune juice in one gulp, without ANY fuss. "Yana even said me and Nisha can enter Chip in the dog show in a few weeks' time."

"Hmm," said Mum. "As long as it doesn't clash with Max and Bunny's wedding. . ."

OH NO!

"I'd almost forgotten about being a bridesmaid," I groaned.

"You'd better not let Bunny hear you say that," warned Mum. "We're seeing her after school tomorrow to have a fitting for your dress. Max will be there later, too. They want you to meet Fifi-Belle."

"Fifi-Belle?" I said. "Who's that? It sounds like a poodle's name."

"Yes," Mum smiled. "Doesn't it just."

CHAPTER 14

Fifi-Belle was not a secret surprise poodle.

"Let me introduce you," said Bunny, when me, Tiff and Mum arrived at the BRIDE YOUR TIME dress shop. Bunny had told Tiff she was too big to be a bridesmaid (not that Tiffany minded). But she had come to the fitting anyway – probably just to laugh at me.

"Fifi-Belle is my niece," said Bunny. "She's going to be my other little bridesmaid along with Violet, remember?"

A girl about two years younger than me stomped out of the dressing room. "Hello. You've got freckles," she said, pointing at my nose.

"And you're ... a girl?" I said, giggling to myself about how I had imagined she might really be a poodle.

"Of course I'm a girl!" Fifi-Belle stamped her foot.

"Honestly, Violet. What did you think she would be?" laughed Tiff. But before I could answer, Mum poked me in the ribs. Why does she always do that whenever Bunny is around?

The funny thing was, Fifi-Belle did look a little bit like a poodle. She had **big blue** eyes, a round nose and a **huge** pink bow on the top of her head. She was wearing little pink ankle socks with fluffy pom-poms on the back.

She didn't seem to think much of me. "You've got short hair," she said. "You look like a boy."

"No I don't."

"Actually, short hair is really stylish at the moment," said Tiffany, which is about the first nice thing she's said about me since . . . well, EVER!

But Fifi-Belle just stuck out her tongue. "Aunt Bunny said I'd be a prettier bridesmaid than you. She was right."

"Don't be silly, Fifi-Belle! I never said anything of the sort," blushed Bunny. "Violet's going to be really pretty, too. Just wait until we've got her out of those funny old dungarees and into a lovely frilly bridesmaid dress."

"There's nothing funny about my dungarees," I spluttered.

"They've got mud on them!" Fifi-Belle pointed to my knees.

I looked down and saw two perfect paw prints. Chip must have jumped up on me yesterday. I had just grabbed the first thing I'd seen to change into today when I got back from school.

"Of course, when I designed the bridesmaid

dress I wasn't really imagining it on Violet," said Bunny. She was whispering to the dressmaker far too loudly. "You see, my ex-boyfriend Tarquin had this little god-daughter with long, long golden hair and. . ."

"Is Violet wearing the same bridesmaid's dress as me?" asked Fifi-Belle. "The pretty one with the big blue frilly petticoats?"

"Of course," said Bunny. "You're both going to be my lovely little shepherdesses. Think of that!"

"I don't want her to be the same," pouted Fifi-Belle. "I want to be your only shepherdess."

"Maybe I could wear something different?" I said.

"Bridesmaid dungarees?" snorted Tiffany.

"Certainly not!" cried Bunny.

"Or perhaps just one bridesmaid would be easier," I said. "I don't mind if... OUCH!"

Mum nudged me in the ribs . . . again.

After we had finished being measured for the dresses, we met up with Dad and Uncle Max. Then we all went out for dinner.

Bunny chose the restaurant. It was called THE BIG GREEN PLATE, which sounds fun. But it wasn't.

Mum was in raw vegetable heaven.

"Can I get you a drink?" said the waiter. "We have orange juice, apple juice, plum juice, carrot juice, turnip juice..."

"Turnip juice?" I giggled.

"One turnip juice," said the waiter.

"No! I don't want one," I said. "I was just..."

But it was too late. He had written the order down and moved on to the next person.

"Don't worry," winked Uncle Max. "I'll get an apple juice. We can always swap."

"Have you got anything fizzy?" said Fifi-Belle. "I only like fizzy drinks."

"Erm ... we have sparkling water," said the waiter.

"I want a *PROPER* fizzy drink!" roared Fifi-Belle, slamming her fist on the table.

"Oh dear." Bunny flapped her arms helplessly in the air. "Why don't you have a lovely juice now and I'll see if I can get you a fizzy drink on the way home?"

"I want a fizzy drink **NOW!**" screamed Fifi-Belle.

*

Ten minutes later, Bunny was still trying to get her out from under the table.

Mum was explaining to Dad and Uncle Max how you could make organic confetti from dried courgette flowers – I don't think either of them were really listening. Tiffany was playing music on her headphones with her hair pulled down over her ears so she thought no one could see.

"Hey, Uncle Max," I cried, looking out of the window. "There's a playground. Want a quick go on the slide?"

"You bet!" Uncle Max was on his feet in a second.

"But you haven't even ordered your food," said Bunny.

I looked at the menu. There seemed to be spinach in every single dish.

"It all sounds so delicious," said Mum.

"I suppose I'll try the **vegetable surprise**," I groaned.

"Me too," Uncle Max grinned. "Let's hope the surprise is, there's no vegetables!"

He roared with laughter. For a moment it was like the old Max was back.

He grabbed my hand. "Come on, ᵴUPER-V! To the slide!"

But the second we moved, Bunny stopped us.

"Don't be silly. You can't go out to the playground, Maxi darling," she said.

"Why?" Uncle Max pretended to stamp his foot and sulk. "I want to go on the swings," he joked.

"Not in your lovely suit," Bunny smiled through her teeth. "The playground will be filthy." She caught hold of his pale blue sleeve.

"Oh... Well... Yes. I suppose you're right."
Uncle Max sat down. All the fun and laughter had
gone from him again – like watching the air sink
out of whoopee cushion.

"Sorry, Vi," he mumbled. "But the trousers are
dry-clean only."

Dry-clean only...? Was this the same man who had driven across the Sahara Desert in his underpants because his shorts were holding the engine together? Was this the same Uncle Max who'd had his socks eaten by a crocodile in the Nile? The man who had made his own coat out of a sleeping bag to walk through the snow in Iceland? Now he wouldn't even go to a playground in case his suit got dirty!

"Sorry, Vi," he muttered again. It was as if **EVIL ZOMBIES** had stolen the real Uncle Max. They had taken **SUPER MAX** and swapped him for Soppy Max The Blue Suit Man.

"Sit down, Maxi darling," said Bunny firmly. "Try the Mixed Grain Platter. That was always Tarquin's favourite..."

CHAPTER 15

In the next three weeks I seemed to spend HOURS in the wedding shop being fitted and measured for the dress. Bunny wanted me and Fifi-Belle to practise a special bridesmaid walk, too. But I still went to PAW THINGS as often as I could.

Sometimes Nisha came with me, but she was busy with cousins who were visiting from London, so most of the time I went on my own. I helped out with all the dogs and the cats. Even Mum was impressed with how hard I was working.

When I was finished with my chores, I always saved time to play with Chip and practise for the Agility Trial.

Yana helped me to set up a little course in the orchard.

There was a short tunnel for Chip to run along, weaving poles to swerve in and out of, a little fence to jump over, a hanging tyre to leap through and a see-saw to run up and down. There was also a square painted on the ground where the dogs were supposed to **STOP** and sit for three seconds. This was called the Pause Box. Yana explained that it was my job to run along beside Chip – with no lead, of course – and encourage him through each of these obstacles.

"It is only a fun agility contest at our show," she said. "Not strict rules. But Lady Valance, the judge, is a very well-known dog-training person. She has trained dogs for kings and queens and presidents."

"Don't worry," I said, trying not to sound nervous. "Chip and I will make you proud."

"Good." Yana smiled and stroked Chip's ears. "I am looking forward to this dog show. It will be my last one."

"Why?" I gasped. I had grown to really like Yana. Even though she looked **WILD** with her **CRAZY** green hair and safety pins in her clothes, she was so gentle and kind with the dogs.

"I am leaving **PAW THINGS** to go back to Russia," she explained. "I have a wonderful chance to work with Siberian wolves in the wild."

"Wow!" I said. "That sounds AMAZING. Perhaps you'll meet the wolf cub I adopted. He's called Boris."

"I'll have to look out for him," Yana laughed.

"But we'll miss you here," I said. "Chip will miss you most of all."

"Oh, that is kind," she said, scratching him on the belly as he rolled over to be tickled. "You will have to win the Agility Trial for me before I go."

"We'll try our very best," I promised.

The trouble was, our very best wasn't very good.

Chip loved running through the tunnel and sometimes went through three or four times in a row. He went under the see-saw more often than he went over it. His legs were so short the jump and tyre had to be really low to the ground. And, no matter how hard I tried, he would **NEVER** sit and wait in the Pause Box.

"Chip, STEADY!

"Chip, SLOW!

"Chip, FASTER!

"Chip, SIT!" I bellowed helplessly. There were so many commands.

By the day before the dog show, I had almost lost my voice.

"It is shouting that has done that," said Yana, when she heard me wheeze on the last evening. "Shouting is not good for you or the dog. Try to keep your voice very small . . . very calm."

"OK," I croaked.

And when Nisha arrived, she found me crawling around the course, whispering in Chip's ear.

"Come on, boy. Steady now," I breathed.

Round we went, me on all fours and Chip

running along on his short legs right beside me.
Over the see-saw he went. In and out of the poles.
And he even sat in the Pause Box for about one and
a half seconds, which was a record.

"You do look funny," said Nisha. "Are you
pretending to be a dog?"

"I'm just explaining things to him calmly,"
I said. "Yana was right. That's the best practice
Chip's ever done. He pays no attention AT

ALL when I shout." I crawled close to his ear, talking very quietly again. "But if I get down on his level and whisper, he's a very good dog."

Chip wagged his tail like mad.

"If only you could do that tomorrow," said Nish. "For the real thing."

"Wouldn't it be brilliant if I could," I said. "But this judge – Lady Valance – is really posh and important. I bet she'd disqualify me if I crawled around on my hands and knees."

Chip rolled on his back, waiting to have his belly tickled.

"We've done enough for today," I said. "That's the best Chip's ever done. We'll just have to wait and see if it is good enough to beat Riley."

"Fingers crossed," said Nisha, but she didn't sound very sure. Whatever kind of dog Speedy was, he was bound to be bigger and faster and more obedient than Chip.

"Do you ever wish you had entered the Agility Trial with ... well, with a different dog?" said Nisha gently.

"You mean instead of Chip? No! Never!" I picked him up and hugged him tightly. "He may be small, and a bit of a rascal ... but Chip's the only dog in the **WHOLE WORLD** for me," I said.

A lump rose in my throat. I realized I didn't mean that just for the Agility Trial. I meant for ever...

"Even if Uncle Max brought me a brand new puppy, I wouldn't want it now," I said, burying my face in Chip's scruffy fur. "Chip is the best dog ever. I wouldn't swap him for anything."

"And he thinks you're the best girl, too," laughed Nish, as Chip stared up at me with his big dark eyes.

"That's why I've got to win the Agility Trial," I said. "It'll prove to Mum I'm responsible enough to handle a dog, and it'll show everybody that me and Chip are the **perfect match**."

"Just one problem," said Nisha.

"Speedy," I groaned.

"Ha! Talk about perfect timing," said a whiny voice, and Riley Paterson appeared from nowhere. His head popped up over the orchard wall like a rat from a hole.

"That's trespassing! Visitors are supposed to report to reception," said Nisha, as he swung his leg over the top.

"How long have you been listening?" I asked.

"Long enough to hear you talking about my dog," he grinned. "You really should see her, you know."

It was obvious Riley had been hanging around on the road outside and climbed up the wall just to taunt us. He was probably trying to spy on me and Chip practising the agility course.

"**L**OSERS!" He made a silly L-shape with his fingers and nearly toppled off the top of the wall. "Worried, are you?" he said, steadying himself and holding on to the bricks more tightly.

"No! Chip will beat your dog any day," I said. "What kind of breed did you say she was?"

"I didn't," said Riley. He swung his leg back over the orchard wall and dropped down on to the street again. "I can't wait till you see her. Save your pocket money," he called. "You're going to need it to buy ten big fat bars of **TOFFAMEL**. All for me!" I heard him laughing as he ran away.

"I don't have any pocket money," I whispered

once he'd gone. "Mum's making me pay her back for losing my wellie."

"Then you'll just have to win," smiled Nisha as we walked back inside and tucked Chip up in his basket for the night.

"Speedy is probably just one of those joke names that means the opposite," I said.

"Like Tiny," nodded Nish as we passed his cage. "He's called that even though he's **HUGE**."

"Exactly," I said. Tiny leapt at the bars as if he was trying eat us. "Speedy has probably only got three legs. She's probably not a dog at all. She's probably a tortoise."

"Or, if she is a dog, she'll be a dainty poodle. Too posh to run about and jump," said Nisha.

But neither of us could imagine Ratty-Riley with a poodle.

Chapter 16

I wanted to arrive at the PAW THINGS DOG SHOW *SUPER* early. But Bunny came round and made me try on six nearly identical pairs of blue satin bridesmaid's slippers to see which she liked best. There was no sign of Uncle Max.

"It's best us girls do all the arrangements together," winked Bunny, trying the very first pair of slippers all over again.

"Will you remind Uncle Max I'm going to be at the dog show later, though? I'm doing an Agility

Trial," I said. "I think he'd really enjoy it and—"

"Maxi doesn't have time for that sort of nonsense," sighed Bunny. "You don't seem to realize, Violet, but the wedding is **NEXT WEEKEND!**"

"But—"

"I shouldn't snap," she said, dabbing at her lips with a frilly hankie. "It's just that everything needs to be so perfect." She gathered up the pale blue slippers. "I've booked Maxi a barber's appointment to have his moustache trimmed this afternoon. Sorry!"

I wish Uncle Max could have come to the dog show. He would have loved it. It was **BRILLIANT**. There were pet shop stalls and information tents all round the edge of the grass in King's Park and a big ring beside the bandstand where the events would happen. As well as the trial, there were breed classes and puppy classes, and even special classes for old dogs called veterans. There was the Dog Who Looks Most Like Its Owner contest, a Sheepdog Display with real sheep and a Sniffer Dog Show from the police.

I saw all kinds, shapes and sizes of AMAZING dogs – a beautiful Hungarian vizsla the colour of marmalade, a tiny papillon with ears like a flying butterfly and an Old English sheepdog with hair even more **FRIZZY** than Tiff's. If I had brought along my Bumper Book Of Dogs I could have scored a zillion points for ticking off so many different breeds. But I had no time for my Bumper Book now. All I could think about was the Agility Trial. I glanced around. No sign of Riley yet.

The competition was due to start in twenty minutes.

But, before that, Nisha was determined to get Chip looking his best. We spread out a rug under a quiet oak tree beside the tennis courts.

"He can't be scruffy in the ring," she explained. "Especially not with someone as fancy as Lady Valance judging. Haven't you ever seen dog shows on the telly? The dogs always look PERFECT. Pass me the brush. . ."

Nisha pointed towards a basket full of grooming things. It looked like she was preparing poor Chip for a fashion show. She had brought along ribbons and bows, brushes and combs, and something called Doggy Delux Super Shine Furspray, which came in a gold bone-shaped can.

"It'll make Chip's coat sparkle." She sprayed a puff behind his ears. "It smells like pomegranate, too," she smiled.

"But does Chip want to smell like pomegranate?" I asked. From the look on Chip's face, he did **NOT!** He wrinkled his little puggy nose and rolled his big black eyes. Nisha took no notice. It's like when we're doing a project at school. Once she gets started, nothing can stop her.

She smoothed down Chip's shaggy brown hair, wiped his face and combed his fluffy ears. She even blew his nose with a tissue and brushed his teeth – which wasn't easy because Chip kept *CHEWING* the bristles off the toothbrush.

She scrubbed and sprayed and rinsed and curled. I hardly recognized poor Chip, he looked so SHINY and CLEAN. Then Nisha tied a

big silver ribbon round his
neck and a pom-pom on
the end of his tail.

"What do you think?"
she asked, glancing
nervously at her watch.
"Ready to go?"

"Erm. . ."

Nisha looked
at me, waiting for an
answer. Chip was looking at me, too.

"Gosh. . . What can I say?" Dogs hate it when
you laugh at them, so I kept my face as straight as I
possibly could. "He looks very . . . different."

"Different is good, isn't it?" said Nisha. "He
was so scruffy before and. . ."

She looked down at Chip, who was trying to

bite the pom-pom off his tail. " **GRRRRRRRRRR!**"
He chased it round and round in circles.

"Oh dear," giggled Nisha. "I've gone too far,
haven't I?"

"Maybe just a bit. . ." I didn't want to tell her
that poor Chip looked like he'd been dressed up in
the doggy version of my **Little Bo FREAK**
bridesmaid's dress.

"I suppose we could take off the bow," said
Nisha.

"And the pom-pom. . .?" I suggested.

Poor Nish – the minute we'd taken all the
ribbons off, Chip rolled on the ground. He
squirmed and scratched until his coat stuck up like
a hedgehog.

That's better! I could just imagine him saying.
Thank goodness that lot has gone. A dog's not

supposed to have ribbons … not a rough, tough dog like me.

"Oh Chip! Come here," scolded Nisha. "I've got to brush you again now. You're all covered in leaves and grass."

"No time for that," I said. "Listen."

The loudspeaker boomed across the park:

WOULD COMPETITORS FOR THE CHILD HANDLER AGILITY TRIAL PLEASE MAKE YOUR WAY TO THE MAIN RING NOW…

I sprang to my feet and glanced round the park.

"Where's Riley?" I said. "Can you see him? If he doesn't get here soon, he's going to miss it."

"Perhaps he isn't coming," said Nisha, hopefully.

"He's probably too scared to face **Chip the Mighty!**" I said, crossing my fingers as we ran towards the main ring. We charged past Mum, who was sipping a cup of herbal tea in the cafe.

"See you there. Dad's buying a programme," she called. "Good luck!"

"I'm going to need it," I panted to Nisha, and we ran on towards the bandstand. "At least the scoreboard says there are only three dogs entered. See? Me and Chip. Someone called Sophy with a dog named Jester. And, of course, Ratty-Riley with Spee..." I stopped dead in my tracks. "Nisha, look."

Riley was standing by the entrance to the show ring.

"Oh no!" Nisha grabbed my arm. "So Speedy wasn't a joke name after all," she groaned.

I shook my head. "Doesn't look like it."

Riley was chatting to a couple of boys from school. Standing next to him was a beautiful silver greyhound!

"She's like a racehorse-dog," I gasped.

Just looking at Speedy you could tell she was *fast*. Tall and fit and lean – she was pulling away from Riley, straining on her lead and pawing at the ground.

Nisha and I ducked behind the programme stand. Riley hadn't spotted us yet.

"Hello, girls." Dad was getting his change.

"Shhh!" I peered round the edge of the stand, trying to get another quick look at Speedy. Riley was still just standing around, chatting to the boys. But Speedy's muscles **rippled** as she pulled on the lead. She was desperate to get into the ring.

"Ah," said Dad, following my gaze. "Stiff competition, I see. The Patersons have kept greyhounds for years. Riley's dad breeds them for racing. Didn't you know?"

"No!" My palms felt sweaty.

If I had known I wouldn't have told Riley I could beat him. He would **NEVER** let me forget this. Worse still, if he beat me, I couldn't prove to Mum and Dad that I'd trained Chip perfectly (or at least enough to keep him out of trouble).

" **RUFF! RUFF!** " Chip jumped up as a girl with a collie came towards the show ring. She squeezed round the side of the programme stand and stood beside us.

"Hi, I'm Sophy," she said as Chip and the collie sniffed each other. She looked about three years older than me, with a lovely big smile and long, straight brown hair. "This is Jester." She ruffled his black and white ears. "We're up first, I think."

Collies are brilliant at agility – they are intelligent and easy to train. . .

"We're in BIG trouble, Nish," I whispered. "Chip won't stand a chance against Jester the BRAINY-BOX collie and Speedy the SUPER-FAST greyhound."

"I really love your dog," smiled Sophy, tickling Chip under the chin. "He's adorable."

"He *is* adorable," I said, furious with myself for being downhearted. I glanced over at Dad who was checking his texts. "Chip's not mine yet, but he will be . . . somehow . . . soon!"

"Fingers crossed," said Nisha.

"Good luck. It's Violet, isn't it?" said Sophy as she hurried towards the entrance to the ring.

"Yes," I whispered, hoping Ratty-Riley wouldn't turn round and see me.

But he did.

"There you are! I thought you'd chickened out," he grinned. He jerked on Speedy's lead so that she lifted her head. "Do you like my dog?"

"Yes," I said truthfully.

"She's very pretty."

"Pretty fast!" roared Riley. He jiggled up and down and looked as if he might wet himself, he thought his joke was so funny. "Are you scared we're going to beat you?"

"No. Not really." I shook my head.

"Well, you should be!" Riley pulled hard on Speedy's lead, winding it around his fist. "Just look at that little guinea pig."

"Chip is NOT a guinea pig," I said.

Riley laughed. "He doesn't even reach to Speedy's knees! Do you really think you can beat a purebred champion greyhound with that?"

"Easy," I said, as Chip rolled on to his back, waiting to have his belly tickled.

"Easy-peasy," agreed Nisha.

But no matter how much we both LOVED Chip, we knew that wasn't true.

CHAPTER 17

As the competition started, Riley ran off to join the boys from school. They were sitting on the bandstand steps.

Nisha and I stayed by the side of the ring with Dad. I watched as Sophy and Jester began the course. He was a lovely old dog with a speckled grey muzzle and flecks of white across his black sheepdog fur.

"Come on, boy," Sophy urged him as she took off his lead and they swung through the starting gate. He ambled forward and wagged his tail.

"He loves this, does Jester," said an old man standing on the other side of Dad. I think he must have been Sophy's grandfather. "He used to be a champion agility dog when he was younger. But he's like me – getting on a bit now. Not as fast as he was."

"He's still doing well, though," said Dad.

It was true. Jester had sprung cleanly over the jump and now Sophy was calling him through the tunnel. Nisha clapped.

"Are you watching?" I said to Chip. "It's through the gate first. Then the jump. Then the tunnel. We need to remember the route. We'll lose points if we go the wrong way."

Chip wagged his tail.

"Good luck, the pair of you," said Dad, patting me on the head and ruffling Chip's ear.

He waved across the ring to Mum, who'd found seats for them under the scoreboard. "We'll be watching."

"This is it, Nish," I said as Dad left us. I kept my eyes fixed on everything Sophy was doing. As Jester reached the white Pause Box painted on the grass, she raised her hand and smiled.

"Stay!" she commanded. Jester sat still as a statue right in the middle of the square. **One second. Two seconds. Three seconds. . .** Then he was off again, heading for the see-saw.

"Don't forget to stop there, Chip." I said, bending to whisper in his ear. "That's when you have to stay very still, remember?"

I knew what Chip would be thinking: *Sitting still is boring*.

"We have to do well," I said. "Especially for Yana." I'd only caught a glimpse of her once or twice since we had arrived at the show. She was busy organizing volunteers, manning the information tent and selling raffle tickets to raise money for **PAW THINGS**. But she'd wished me luck this morning when I had collected Chip.

"There she is!" I saw the top of her green spiky hair over by the bandstand. She rattled her donation tin but Riley and the boys shook their heads and ignored her.

When he wasn't sniggering and pointing at Chip, Riley was running up and down the grass with Speedy. He kept making her sit and sprint, just to show how fast she could go. He wasn't even watching to see how well Jester handled the course or to try and learn the route.

"That dog is ancient," was all I heard him say as the old collie took a slow run-up and $j^{um}p_{ed}$ stiffly through the hanging tyre.

It was true. Jester wasn't fast. But he was careful. He hadn't knocked a single obstacle – not even with his thick, wagging tail. And now, for one last tricky test – the weaving poles.

Jester trotted slowly and calmly through, glancing from side to side as he wound his way steadily between the posts.

"Perfect!" Nisha and I clapped as he crossed the finish line and completed a clear round.

"That's going to be hard for us to beat, Chip," I said. But I was pleased for Sophy. She had been so friendly and Jester was a lovely old dog.

LET'S HAVE A ROUND OF APPLAUSE FOR JESTER AND SOPHY!

the loudspeaker boomed.

A CLEAR ROUND WITH A FINAL
SCORE OF EIGHT OUT OF TEN …
JUST LOSING TWO POINTS FOR
BEING SLIGHTLY OUTSIDE OF THE
TIME LIMIT, I'M AFRAID.

"Eight out of ten," said Nisha. "That's good, right?"

"It's brilliant," I agreed.

"Then let's just hope Riley and Speedy make

a mess of it," said Nisha. "As long as you can beat

them, that's the main thing."

"Exactly," I agreed, but the loudspeaker

drowned me out.

LADIES AND GENTLEMEN …
JUST TAKE A LOOK AT OUR NEXT COMPETITOR –
A BEAUTIFUL FOUR-YEAR-OLD RACING GREYHOUND.
SPEEDY BY NAME, SPEEDY BY NATURE.
DON'T THINK WE'LL HAVE ANY TROUBLE
WITH THE TIME LIMIT HERE…

Riley unclipped Speedy's lead and she shot into the ring like a rocket.

"See you later, Violet," he grinned. "Don't forget to buy those **TOFFAMELS**!"

"I'd like to stuff those **TOFFAMELS** up his nose," I growled to Nisha.

"I know. He's so full of himself," she said, picking the twigs out of Chip's coat and smoothing down his ears. "You'd think he already won the trial!"

"He might as well have done," I said. "Look!"

As the whistle blew, Speedy flew through the starting gate and leapt over the first jump like a stag.

Riley had to hitch up his jogging trousers and sprint to keep up.

"Faster, Speedy. Faster," he panted, scrambling along behind her as she bounded towards the tunnel.

I thought for a moment she might swerve and miss it, but she slid herself through and popped from the other end like a champagne cork.

"Come on!" screamed Riley, punching the air and running towards the see-saw.

Speedy hesitated for a moment, turning her head towards the white square painted on the grass beside her.

"She knows what to do," I whispered. "It's the Pause Box next."

But Riley thought he knew better. **"COME ON, SPEEDY!** Get on the see-saw, you silly dog!"

With one last glance, Speedy lurched forward and followed his call. The crowd gasped.

"What it is?" said Nisha.

"She's supposed to sit for three seconds," I said. "But Riley made her run on. I knew he should have watched what Sophy and Jester did."

In one bound Speedy was up and over the see-saw, and before I could blink, she had sped on and jumped through the hanging tyre, too.

"What happens if you go wrong on the course?" said Nisha.

"I'm not sure," I said, leaping up and down.

I clapped my hands as a tiny bubble of hope grew inside me. "I think it means we might be in with a chance. It means Riley can't get a perfect score."

Seconds later, Speedy had finished the course, gliding through the weaving poles so fast she looked more like flowing water than a dog.

Riley ran in a circle and threw his arms up in the air like a footballer scoring a goal.

"Yes!" he cried, cheering to all the boys at the side of the ring. He still had no idea he had missed the Pause Box out, but he hadn't even bothered to pat Speedy or tell her how well she had done.

A GOOD FAST ROUND...

announced the loudspeaker.

BUT POINTS WILL BE DEDUCTED FOR MISSING OUT THE PAUSE BOX, I'M AFRAID.

"What? That's stupid!" Riley stood in the middle of the ring and shook his fist in the air.

SO THAT GIVES A FINAL SCORE TO SPEEDY AND RILEY OF ... EIGHT OUT OF TEN.

"Yes!" I clapped my hands and cheered. That was the same score as Sophy and Jester. Brilliant. Riley wasn't in the lead. "He's still going to be tough to beat," I said, crouching down and throwing my arms around Chip's neck. "But we've got a chance. Not a very big chance, but a . . . Oh no!"

Suddenly, I wasn't crouching down with my arms thrown around Chip's neck any more. I was tiny and clinging on to his collar for dear life.

I'd shrunk so fast this time, I didn't even feel my toes tingle.

"Violet?" said Nisha somewhere far above me.

"Where are you?"

"Down here," I called. But she couldn't hear me.

The loudspeaker boomed above me.

COULD WE PLEASE HAVE
OUR FINAL CONTESTANT.
THAT'S VIOLET POTTS AND CHIP.
PLEASE COME TO THE RING NOW.

My tiny head was spinning. If I couldn't get back to full size and quickly, I couldn't take Chip in the ring. We would have to miss the trial.

CHAPTER 18

As the loudspeaker blared out my name, Riley came over and looked down at Chip.

"Ha!" he said. For a moment I thought he had seen me clinging on to the little red collar. But he turned to Nisha. "Has Violet run away? Has she chickened out of the trial?"

"No." Nisha put her hands on her hips and tried to look tough, but I could tell she was panicking. "Violet will be here ... soon." She glanced down, looking amongst people's feet. Poor Nisha must have guessed I'd shrunk, but she had no idea where I was.

I wanted to wave at her, but I daren't in case Ratty-Riley saw me. He is the last person in the **WHOLE ENTIRE WORLD** I would want to see me tiny. He'd probably catch me and pickle me in a jar. He's always showing off about how he did that to a frog.

"She better hurry up or she's going to miss her turn," grinned Riley as the loudspeaker boomed out my name again.

THIS IS A FINAL CALL FOR VIOLET POTTS. PLEASE COME TO THE RING NOW.

I had to do something! Mum and Dad would be wondering where I was, too. They'd think it was really irresponsible not to show up once I had entered the competition. Perhaps I'd lose my chance to keep Chip for ever.

IF ANYONE KNOWS THE WHEREABOUTS OF VIOLET POTTS OR CHIP, CAN THEY PLEASE COME TO THE RING AND TELL US...

"Oh dear," breathed Nisha. She scooped Chip up and put him under her arm.

"Really doesn't seem to be coming, does she?" said Riley. "I'll go and tell the judges. S'pose she'll be disqualified. It's no big deal."

"Wait," said Nisha, still peering at the ground. "She'll be round here ... somewhere!" But Riley had sped off.

"NISH," I shouted, dangling from Chip's collar. "Eeeek!" I squeaked, hoping she would recognize my little mousey call.

Chip flicked his ear in excitement as he heard me squeak.

"That's it!" I cried. "Good boy, Chip!" He wagged his tail again, turning his head to try and see me. This time Nisha heard me, too. She looked down and her eyes widened as she spotted me clinging to Chip's collar. "Violet!"

She lifted Chip higher as if she was adjusting his collar. "Oh Violet, this is terrible," she gasped. "You won't be able to do the agility trial now you've shrunk."

"But I've had an idea!" She was so close she could hear me clearly. "It's brilliant – super-double-choc brilliant – don't you see?" I grinned. "Chip just heard me squeak! If I stay tucked up, I can whisper in his ear and he'll do exactly as I say. It'll be even BETTER than when I crawled along beside him."

THIS REALLY IS THE LAST CHANCE FOR VIOLET POTTS AND CHIP...

"Quick! Before Riley tells the judges we're not coming," I said.

"You'll have to take Chip into the ring. He needs to have a handler."

"But I don't know the course," said Nisha. "You know I haven't practised."

"Leave that to me and Chip," I said as I scrambled up his collar and hid behind his ear.

"Go!" I cried.

I watched Riley striding towards the judges' table. I knew which one was Lady Valance at once from her huge feathery hat.

"Excuse me," he called. "Violet Potts isn't . . ."

". . . isn't able to be here," said Nisha bravely, running up alongside him. "But she has trained this dog all by herself." Nish was shouting loud enough for the crowd to hear. "And I am going to show you what he can do." She unclipped his lead.

"RUFF! RUFF! RUFF!" Chip leapt out of her arms. I had to cling on tight to a tuft of his fur to stop myself flying through the air.

"Come on, Chip," I whispered in his ear. "Time for a LITTLE FUN!"

Chip sped into the middle of the ring.

WELL, WELL! WHAT A FUNNY LITTLE DOG. . .

the voice on the loudspeaker chuckled.

"Little or not, we'll show them," I said, leaning forward and whispering right into Chip's ear again. "I'm here with you."

And just like that, Chip shot through the starting gate and we were off.

"Steady," I whispered.

"Good boy." Nisha ran along beside us. But I knew Chip wasn't really listening to her. It was my quiet little voice in his ear that he liked. All I had to do was whisper gently and he would do anything I said. Yana was right – dogs hate being shouted at. I know how they feel! Bunny kept shouting at me when I was practising the special slow bridesmaid walk she wanted. Whenever she yelled I just panicked and tripped over my own feet.

"Yippee for shrinking," I laughed, hidden deep in the

thick hair around Chip's neck. "Now we really do make the perfect team!"

Chip sped up to the first obstacle.

"Jump!" I whispered, and up he leapt through the air.

UP! UP! UP!

He flew over the jump! (It had been lowered a bit since Jester and Speedy, but that was fair. In a real agility trial, like the ones you see on the telly, Jester and Speedy would have been counted as big breeds. Chip was only a mini-size dog.)

"Just like me. I'm mini too!" I giggled as we landed safely on the far side of the jump.

I felt like a tiny circus rider – and I was L♡VING the ride.

"ROLL UP! ROLL UP!" I laughed. "COME SEE THE AMAZING FLYING CHIPOLATA AND HIS FAMOUS mini RIDER – VIOLET POTTS, THE smallest GIRL IN THE WORLD!"

Chip slowed for a second as if he was trying to figure out what I was saying.

"Go!" I cried, not wanting to confuse him. "Keep on."

We shot down the middle of the tunnel, which was a bit like a real big-top tent at a circus, with its bright red and yellow stripes high above our heads.

"Good boy." I patted Chip's neck, holding on tight, as we charged out of the tunnel again and into the bright spring sunlight.

"Well done!" said Nisha, looking around for where to go next.

The crowd cheered as the loudspeaker spoke over them.

THIS LITTLE FELLOW REALLY IS GOING FLAT OUT...

"Now this is the tricky one," I warned, leaning hard into Chip's neck to try and urge him over to the left. "It's the Pause Box. . ."

As soon as we were inside the square, I spoke as calmly and clearly as I could. "SIT, CHIP! STAY!"

Chip sat. I couldn't believe it – he was doing exactly as I told him to. He had **NEVER** been this obedient before. **One second. Two seconds. Three seconds. . .**

"GO, CHIP! GO!" I cried, and away he roared as soon as the three seconds were over.

Riding the see-saw was awesome.

top we charged.

the   Then

to

Up   W

H

E

E!

Down the other side we flew.

If only I could always be tiny enough to whisper in his ear, Chip would be the best-behaved dog in the universe.

GREAT SHOW!

cheered the voice on the loudspeaker.

We shot past the judges' chairs and Lady Valance nodded her head so that the feathers on her hat wobbled like a dancing peacock.

As we galloped towards the tyre hanging from its tree, I glanced backwards. Nisha was running to keep up. Behind her I could see the big clock above the scoreboard. We were making *SUPER-QUICK* time. We hadn't knocked down a single obstacle or missed anything out – not even the tiniest mistake. If we carried on like this, it might just be possible. We might beat Riley after all.

OK, so Mum and Dad wouldn't know I was actually here guiding Chip round the ring. But at least they'd see how well I'd trained him.

"JUMP!" I cried, and we leapt up through the hanging tyre. Looking up, I caught a glimpse of a squirrel as it scurried through the branches of the tree above us.

"Good boy," I breathed as we landed on the grass again. "You're going to be the champion, Chip!" I sang in his ear as we thundered on. "Just the weaving poles left."

But, as I turned to glance at the clock again, my heart thumped. The squirrel had scampered down from the tree now. It swung upside down from the tyre and dropped on to the grass behind us.

If Chip got even a sniff of squirrel scent, we were **SUNK!**

"No!" I cried as he turned his head towards it. We were halfway through the weaving poles already. All we had to do was get to the end.

"NO, CHIP! NAUGHTY!" I tried my strictest voice,

but once Chip has seen a squirrel, NOTHING can stop him!

" **RUFF!** " he barked.

The squirrel fled.

Nisha must have sensed trouble. She grabbed at the lead hanging round her neck, as if she was going to clip it back on.

But it was too late.

Chip charged after the fleeing squirrel.

"Stop!" I cried, clinging on to his collar for dear life. "PLEASE, CHIP! STOP!"

Chapter 19

The squirrel took one look at Chip and bolted straight across the ring.

Chip charged after it.

"We need to finish the course," I cried weakly.

But I knew it was hopeless. Nothing in the world would stop him now. I couldn't believe how fast his little legs could run.

I bounced about like a dangly toy on a car mirror. The squirrel shot under the judges' table. We were so close behind, Chip almost caught it by the tail.

" RUFF! RUFF! RUFF! "

"SIT, BOY!" cried Lady Valance, peering from under her big feathery hat. She leant down and tried to grab Chip. But. . .

" RUFF!"

He took a bite of the feathers, snatched the hat in his jaws and sped on.

Oh no! This was getting worse and worse. . .

"Why did it have to be *her* hat?" I groaned.

For a minute, I couldn't see anything as the feathers bobbed about in front of my face, flapping like an angry peacock.

I scrambled higher up Chip's collar just in time to see us run between Speedy's legs. And there was Riley, bent over double from laughing so much.

But Speedy had spotted the squirrel, too. She pulled the lead from Riley's hand and ran beside us.

"Hey! Come back," cried Riley.

Speedy yapped madly at the squirrel. I remembered what it said in my **Bumper Book Of Dogs**. Greyhounds are trained to race by following a furry electronic toy rabbit on a string. Speedy seemed to think the squirrel was the same thing.

"Look out!" I called to the squirrel. "Climb a tree!" But the animal ran on in a straight line across the park. Chip and Speedy weaved between benches, baby buggies and picnic rugs to try and catch it. This was a new agility course for them ... and much more fun than the real one.

All chance of returning to the ring was lost – we'd never be able to finish the proper Agility Trial now.

Since Speedy has joined us, Chip was running faster than ever.

Speedy was barking but Chip still had the judge's hat clenched firmly in his teeth. At last, the squirrel ran up the side of the cafe and shot on to the roof.

Speedy stopped barking. She stood still, lifting her graceful neck to stare at where the squirrel had gone.

Chip stood on his hind legs and danced from side to side, leaping in the air to try and see it too.

Where'd it go? Where'd it go? I could imagine him saying.

Chip raced in wild circles. It was like being on a fast spinning ride at the fair. My fingers slipped from his collar.

"Help!" I grabbed hold of the hat.

"RUFF!"

As Chip opened his mouth to bark, the hat flew out of his jaws and **spun through the air**. I flew with it, clinging on to a long red feather as I soared through the sky.

The hat hovered like a frisbee for a moment, then dropped down as it skidded to a stop underneath a cafe table.

"Ouch." I hit the ground hard. The hat flopped down on top of me like a giant collapsing umbrella. As I peered out, rubbing my knees, I saw Ratty-Riley's smelly grey trainers running over.

He grabbed hold of Speedy's lead. I could see her thin grey legs where she was still standing waiting for the squirrel to come down from the roof.

I saw Nisha's white pumps sprinting along, too.

"Chip, come here!" she cried.

Chip's hairy little paws danced from left to right just a metre away from the cafe table.

"Stay, boy!" begged Nisha as Yana's electric green lace-up boots came running into view.

At least she'd be able to catch Chip. But I wished she hadn't seen all the commotion. She must have come running from the information tent to help. She'd think that I wasn't here. That I hadn't wanted to do the Agility Trial. That I hadn't looked after Chip properly.

"Sit!" she said. Her hand stretched out.

But Chip dodged sideways. He was still so excited about the squirrel, he wasn't even listening to Yana.

He ran straight between a little girl's pink legs.

SPLA T! Her ice cream fell to the ground.

"Hey!" The girl stamped her foot. All I could see were her ankles, but I'd have recognized those pom-pom socks anywhere. I'd been following them up and down for days on end as we practised our bridesmaid walk. . .

Fifi-Belle!

"Oh no!" I smiled. She'd said she might come to see the dog show, but I didn't think she was really interested.

"HORRID LITTLE DOG!" she roared as Chip stuck his nose in the spilled vanilla and licked his chops.

"Naughty Chip," I whispered, but my voice suddenly grew louder. I shot back to FULL SIZE and banged my head on the table above me.

"Violet!
There you are.
Thank goodness,"
said Nisha, her eyes
wide, as I poked my
head out from
between the chairs.
"I thought you might
have been trampled or. . ."

"Shhh!" I put my finger to my lips. "I'm fine.
It was an awesome ride," I whispered.

"Kindly give me back my hat," snapped
Lady Valance. She snatched it from where it was
perched, lopsided, on my head.

Yana clipped a lead on to Chip.

"I want a new ice cream," sulked Fifi-Belle.

"Violet?" cried Mum, running up and seeing me still halfway out from underneath the table. "What is going on here?"

"Just a bit of trouble with Chip," I sighed.

"It seems there's always trouble with Chip," said Mum.

"He'll be disqualified from the Agility Trial, that's for sure," said Lady Valance. "We allowed you to change the handler at the last minute, but we can't allow for this."

"Ha!" Riley punched the air.

"If a dog doesn't finish the course, we will not award it any points," said Lady Valance, pulling the soggy chewed hat firmly on to her head. It no longer looked like a peacock – more like a dead chicken.

"So I win!" shouted Riley.

"Yes. I suppose you do," Lady Valance nodded. "Joint first place along with Jester, the old collie."

"That's ten **TOFFAMEL** bars you owe me, Violet," Riley crowed.

"All right, all right," I groaned.

"It's a shame," said Lady Valance, "because your little dog was doing surprisingly well."

"That had nothing to do with Violet," said Riley. "She wasn't even there."

"It shows how well I trained him, though. Doesn't it?" I said, smiling hopefully at Mum.

"I'm afraid it shows me you're not responsible enough to be in the right place at the right time," Mum sighed. "Where were you, Violet?"

"Oh . . . it's a very long story," I said. The hope

melted inside me quicker than the spilled ice cream in the sun.

How could everything have gone so wrong?

Riley had won the competition and Mum thought I was more irresponsible than ever.

"You shouldn't make silly bets, Violet," she said. "How are you going to buy Riley those **TOFFAMEL** bars? You still owe me for the wellington boots . . . and now a new ice cream for Fifi-Belle, too."

"I'll have three scoops of toffee crunch with chocolate sprinkles on top, please," smirked Fifi-Belle. "Oh, and strawberry sauce. That's ten pence extra."

"You should count yourself lucky you don't have to pay for that judge's hat as well," said Mum as we watched Lady Valance storm back to the ring.

Even Yana looked cross as she picked up Chip to take him to the **PAW THINGS** information tent.

"I'd better keep him with me," she said.

"If only it hadn't been for that squirrel! You were doing BRILLIANTLY," I said, reaching to scratch Chip between the ears. A lump rose in my throat. "Goodbye. . ."

Everything was ruined. Mum definitely wouldn't let me get a dog now. Especially not Chip. She thought he was trouble on four short legs. And she thought I could never be trusted to have a dog of my own.

CHAPTER 20

All week I begged Mum to let me go to *PAW THINGS* after school. But we were always busy getting ready for the wedding on Saturday. Bunny called every evening with something else we needed to do.

On Monday I had to have **ANOTHER** fitting for the dress. They even measured my wrists!

On Tuesday I had to have a haircut.

On Wednesday I had to have **ANOTHER**

haircut because Bunny said the first one looked scruffy. (Mum didn't even poke me in the ribs when I complained.)

On Thursday I had to have my nails painted. Bunny took us to a really posh nail bar in town. I wanted each fingernail a different colour – red, orange, yellow, green, blue, indigo, violet, black, white and gold. But Bunny said they all had to be . . . pale blue, of course.

At last, on Friday, I was free. Nish had a piano lesson but Dad dropped me off at PAW THINGS after school.

"Hello," said Yana, as I ran into the kennels. She was brushing Tiny, who didn't even bark at me any more. "I was hoping you would come sooner."

"I'm sorry," I said. "I've been really busy. You see, I'm going to be a bridesmaid tomorrow."

I wriggled my painted fingernails at her. "And... Oh, never mind. Can I just go and visit Chip?"

"Well," said Yana. "You see—"

"Please," I begged. "I'll come back and help with any chores you want me to do. Even cleaning Tiny's teeth!" I joked.

"The thing is—" said Yana.

"I won't be a minute," I promised, charging away down the corridor before Yana could say anything else. I didn't want anyone to stop me from seeing Chip. Not after all this time. I wanted to tell him that no matter what had happened at the Agility Trial, he was still a true CHAMPION to me.

"Violetta! Wait," called Yana. But I was already standing in front of Chip's cage.

Except it wasn't Chip's cage ... not any more.

A little Yorkshire terrier was staring up at me.

"Where's Chip?" I cried.

"I was trying to tell you," said Yana, coming in behind me. "Chip has gone away."

"Gone away?" I breathed.

"A nice, handsome young man came on Monday. He liked Chip very much," smiled Yana. "We checked it is a good home and he adopted Chip. They left just an hour ago."

" **NO!** " I felt my legs go wobbly.

"All week I was hoping you would come," said Yana. "But you didn't."

"All because of the stupid, stupid wedding!" I wailed.

Yana put her arm around my shoulders.

"Ohh!" I felt as if my heart would break.

Violet Potts does not cry ... not normally.

But now tears were streaming down my face.

Chip was gone. I would never see him again. I hadn't even got to say goodbye . . . or to tickle his tummy one last time.

When I got up the next morning, Mum had to pat some of her face powder on my cheeks.

"Oh, Vi," she said, hugging me. "You're all blotchy because you've been crying so much. You really did love that funny little dog, didn't you?"

"Yes," I sniffed.

Mum rocked me in her arms without saying anything for a long time. At last, she dried my eyes and said, "Come on now. It's time to get dressed for the wedding. Bunny won't like it if your eyes are red and puffy."

"No, she won't," I said, and I blew my nose loudly.

Sure enough, Bunny was in terrible state by the time we arrived at the hotel where we were getting ready. One of the one hundred and fifty bows on her enormous meringue wedding dress had fallen off, and the dressmaker had actually crawled right under Bunny's huge frilly skirt to sew it back on.

Fifi-Belle was throwing a tantrum because the bouquet of plastic flowers I had to carry was bigger than hers.

"I'll swap if you like," I said. But she was screeching so loud she didn't hear me.

"Just put your frock on, Violet," snapped Bunny, as if it was my fault that Fifi-Belle was screaming.

I wanted to scream, too. I wanted to yell and shout that someone had taken Chip from me. But it wouldn't do any good. He was gone now. And this was Uncle Max's BIG DAY. He wanted to marry Bunny, even if I couldn't understand why. I would try and make the best of it for him.

"You'll see your shepherdess crook over there by the wall," said Bunny. "It's the one with. . ."

". . .pale blue ribbons?" I guessed.

"Yes," Bunny smiled. Perhaps she felt bad for snapping at me, because she laid her hand on my arm and gave it a squeeze. "Thank you for being our bridesmaid," she said. "I know it means a lot to my darling Tarquin."

"Tarquin?" I said. "What's Tarquin got to do with it?"

"Maxi! I mean my darling Maxi!" Bunny **blushed** as red as her bouquet of plastic roses. "I just got muddled for a moment. You see, I was going to marry Tarquin for so long and then. . . Anyway, what I wanted to say is that we've got you a little present to say thank you for being our bridesmaid. It's waiting for you at WORLD OF WEDDINGS."

"Brilliant," I said. It was probably a box of pale blue frilly hankies if Bunny had chosen it . . . but it was kind of her anyway.

"It's only something tiny," she said. "But I know you'll think it's adorable."

"Thank you," I said, turning towards the mirror.

" **YIKES!** " I didn't mean to but I gasped out loud – there I was looking exactly like the **Little Bo FREAK** bridesmaid picture.

Tiffany popped her head around the door and collapsed in fits of laughter.

"Look at you," she snorted.

I had never tried on the finished dress until now – it hadn't had all the bows and frills sewn on at the final fitting. And I'd never worn the bonnet before either.

Now all that was showing was my round, freckled face. The rest of me – from head to foot – had disappeared as if I were drowning in a deep, frothy sea of pale blue lace.

"You look like a toilet roll holder," squealed Tiffany, holding the door frame so she didn't fall over from laughing. "You know, those ones where you put the loo paper under the skirt."

"Shhh," hissed Mum. "That's not kind."

But a moment later it was my turn to laugh.

"Ah, Tiffany! Thank goodness," exclaimed Bunny, seeing her in the doorway. "I've got the perfect job for you. My best friend was supposed to do it, but she woke up this morning covered in spots. She's refusing to leave the house. So I need you to be my best friend now, Tiff. I need you to be my HAPPY GREETER."

"Happy Greeter?" said Tiffany.

"I want you to stand by the door dressed as a sunflower and make sure that everybody feels DINGLEY DELL happy," smiled Bunny.

"A sunflower?" choked Tiffany.

"WORLD OF WEDDINGS lent me the costume." Bunny sighed as if Tiff was being very stupid. "It's all part of my Dingley Dell country meadow theme. And with your lovely frizzy hair, it'll be perfect."

225

"My hair is **NOT** frizzy!" screamed Tiffany. I thought she was going to stamp her feet like Fifi-Belle.

Bunny ignored her and clicked her fingers for the hairdresser. "Anton, do you have a minute to do that sunflower look we talked about? I want it really high and fluffy and big."

"And **EXTRA frizzy!**" I giggled as the hairdresser led poor Tiffany away.

CHAPTER 21

At eleven o'clock, everyone except the bride and bridesmaids went on ahead to the wedding in their own cars. I caught a glimpse of Tiffany as she ducked out of the door wearing a dress the colour of custard.

Bunny, Fifi-Belle and I followed a few minutes later in a pale blue bridal minibus, which was covered in pale blue ribbons and a pale blue bumper sticker which said:

BRIDE ON BOARD

"Go in and have a peek, Violet," said Bunny when we drew up outside WORLD OF WEDDINGS. It was a large modern building which looked exactly like the big supermarket on the other side of the roundabout. Except instead of having posters saying "baked beans: buy one get one free", WORLD OF WEDDINGS had a big pink love heart which flashed on and off like an electric valentine.

"Just pop your head round the door, Violet," said Bunny. "See if Tarquin is there yet."

"You mean see if Uncle Max is there?" I corrected.

"Him too, of course," said Bunny. "But Tarquin is a sort of guest of honour, you see. He promised he'd come. You can't miss him. He should be sitting right in the front row with his mother – she'll be wearing a lovely big hat with feathers. And his father will be there, too. Did I tell you, his father is a lord? They're ever so rich, you know."

"All right. I'll go and look," I said, climbing out of the minibus – which wasn't easy in my **puffy** dress.

As I pulled my plastic crook out from under the seat, I nearly asked Bunny why she didn't marry Tarquin, seeing as she was always talking about him? But it seemed a bit rude ... after all, in a few minutes' time she was due to marry Uncle Max.

"Don't look so worried, Violet," said Bunny. "It's going to be a wonderful day. The perfect **DINGLEY DELL** wedding! Don't forget, you're getting your little present, so no peeking in any boxes when you go inside. Just have a quick look at who is there and come back and tell me."

"I want a present too," whined Fifi-Belle.

"You'll get one," I heard Bunny say as I hitched up my skirt and hurried across the car park.

I could see Tiffany waiting by the door, dressed as the jolly sunflower ... but she did NOT look jolly. The custard yellow dress was as tight as a sock and her hair was huge. It had been frizzed up to look like giant petals.

"Don't say a word, Little Miss Toilet Roll," she warned, pointing at my Bo Freak dress. "At least I don't look like I've lost my sheep."

"OK, sis. We're in this together," I said. But I couldn't resist one tiny snigger. I remembered what Tiffany had said about getting new hair straighteners if I got a dog.

"You could really do with those straighteners now," I grinned.

Tiffany said something **VERY RUDE**. It was a good job Mum didn't hear or it would have cost at least a pound for the family swear box.

Just inside WORLD OF WEDDINGS was a small waiting room. It was painted bright pink and big fat baby angels hung from the ceiling playing golden trumpets.

In the far corner of the room was a basket – like a big picnic hamper. It was all tied up with pale blue ribbons and a big pale blue bow.

Gosh! Perhaps that's my present, I thought. But I hurried on. I'd be good. I wouldn't look. Not now.

The door to the main hall was ajar and I

could just make out some of the Dingley Dell decorations – a corner of green plastic grass and the edge of a tinfoil pond with rubber water lilies. Above the chatter of the waiting guests, I could hear the sound of the recorded birdsong being played through the speakers. I was about to peek inside and see if I could work out which of the guests was Tarquin when I heard a small, soft whimpering sound.

At first, I thought it was more birdsong, or perhaps a pretend ribbit from a plastic frog, but the noise was coming from somewhere behind me.

I turned round and listened. There it was again. It was DEFINITELY a whimpering sound and it was coming from inside the hamper.

"Hello?" I whispered, moving closer. The noise was getting louder.

It didn't sound like a frog any more.

It sounded like . . . a dog.

"Who's there?" I said softly, my heart thumping.

But, as I crouched down beside the basket and peered through the holes, I heard a sound I would recognize anywhere.

"RUFF!"

"Chip!" I cried, scrabbling to untie the ribbons. I knew I shouldn't be opening the basket but I couldn't help myself. "Chip, is that you?"

"RUFF! RUFF!"

I threw back the lid.

It was him! My Chip! He was staring up at me with his little puggy nose and his deep black eyes. And . . . WHOOSH!

The minute I saw him I shrank with sheer joy.

"Oh, Chip!" I exclaimed, toppling over backwards like a domino. (Thank goodness for the soft, fluffy pink carpet to fall on.)

Now I was in trouble – the wedding was due to start any minute. I couldn't follow Bunny up the aisle if I was the size of a wedding cake decoration.

Even so, I just couldn't help smiling.

"What are you doing here, Chip?" I cried as he leapt out of the basket and snuffled me with his nose.

"ACHOO!" he sneezed as the frills on my

234

(now tiny) **Little Bo FREAK** dress tickled his whiskers.

"Are you here for me?" I couldn't stop the WONDERFUL, **UNBELIEVABLE**, *CRAZY* idea that was growing inside me. "You're not my gift from Bunny, are you? She did say my present would be in the waiting room."

But as soon as I'd thought it, I knew it was silly. No one would buy someone a dog just for being their bridesmaid. But then, it wasn't just for being a bridesmaid, was it? Uncle Max had promised he would get me a dog one day. And Mum had seen how much I loved Chip. Perhaps she had finally given in. Perhaps it was all agreed and Chip was really going to be mine!

"WOW!" If I hadn't shrunk from excitement already, I would have done now.

"Of course you're for me," I said, flinging my arms

around Chip's stubby front leg as he towered above me. From down here, he looked like one of those **shaggy** Scottish cows you see on biscuit tins. I buried my head in his fur. "You must be my present or it wouldn't make ANY sense. Why else would you be here? My Chip. . ."

I hitched up my puffy skirt and was about to do a tiny cartwheel across the floor when I heard Bunny's voice outside the door.

"Tiffany, have you seen Violet?" she hissed. "She was supposed to go in and have a peek. But she's been ages. . ."

I saw the door push slowly open.

"Quick, Chip! Basket!" I hissed.

Luckily Bunny couldn't see him yet. It took her a moment to come in. Her big meringue dress was so **BIG** and so puffy she had turn round and SQUEEZE through the door sideways.

"Basket!" I whispered again, standing on tiptoe so my voice would reach Chip's ear. I couldn't believe it. Chip actually obeyed me – talking in a nice small voice really does work.

As he jumped inside the hamper, I pulled on the end of a ribbon to slam the lid shut.

"Stay, boy," I whispered, still hanging on to the end of the ribbon as it dangled outside the basket.

I had to hide before Bunny saw that I was tiny.

"Geronimo!" I mouthed silently to myself as I leapt off the end of the ribbon like it was a rope swing. I spun sideways, flying through the air. I was trying to land behind the ruffled gold curtains, but I went too far and slipped down inside a pale blue paper bag that I hadn't noticed before.

"Where is Violet?" said Bunny's voice above

me. I could see her peeping through the crack in the door to the main hall. The guests in the Dingley Dell were getting restless.

"We need to go in," said Bunny, starting to sound panicked.

Oh dear! Now Fifi-Belle will have to be a bridesmaid on her own, I thought.

I knew everyone would be furious. Bunny's BIG DAY would be ruined if it didn't go exactly to plan. Uncle Max would be so disappointed. And Mum would say I was irresponsible ... **AGAIN!**

Perhaps I wouldn't be allowed to keep Chip after all.

I wriggled helplessly inside the bag. Something hard and sharp fell against my shoulder.

"Ouch!" As I turned, I found myself staring into

a pair of pale blue glass eyes. They belonged to a small china shepherdess. She was exactly the same height as me and wearing her own **Little Bo FREAK** dress!

CHAPTER 22

I pushed the china shepherdess upright again.

"Sorry," I whispered. She had a little bonnet just like mine, too.

I think she was supposed to look sweet and pretty but she gave me the creeps with her pale, staring eyes.

I didn't have long to look at her, though. A moment later, we both fell out of the bag, t^um^{bl}ing to the floor as Bunny swooped past and knocked us over with her **enormous** dress.

"Ow!" I banged my knee on the edge of the door frame and there was a nasty **cracking** sound like chipping china. I saw that the poor shepherdess's crook had snapped in half.

"I can't wait for Violet any longer," said Bunny. She had no idea, of course, that she had almost **STOMPED** on me.

"You'll have to hold my train by yourself, Fifi-Belle. Don't forget your special slow bridesmaid walk as you follow me up the aisle."

"But I don't want to be on my own," said Fifi-Belle. "I want Violet to—"

"There's no time to argue," said Bunny. "The music is starting."

Sure enough, the sound of birdsong stopped and the **da da dada** wedding music blared out of the speakers.

In his basket, Chip gave a tiny bark.

"Is that you coughing, Fifi-Belle?" said Bunny. "Stop it. You'll ruin the ceremony."

Bunny spun round. I was knocked to the floor again and carried forward as the long train on her wedding dress scooped me up. I struggled to escape but it was no good. I was caught like a leaf in a river of frills.

Bunny took a last glance around the waiting room.

"All set," she said. But as she stepped towards the big door to the main hall, she stopped quite still for a moment and said the strangest thing.

"Oh Tarquin, why isn't it you?" she sighed, wringing her hands.

I **FROZE**, staring up at her from amongst the lace.

"What do you mean, Auntie Bunny?" gasped Fifi-Belle.

"Oh, nothing. I just hope I've done enough," Bunny said, pushing her shoulders back. Her voice sounded choked. "I hope when Tarquin sees this perfect Dingley Dell wedding – the one we always planned – he realizes what he is missing out on. . ."

Da da dada! Da da dada. . .

The music swelled as Bunny pushed open the door and swished down the aisle.

"STOP!" I cried. My mouth was so full of frills it sounded like SWOP! Nobody could hear me anyway as my tiny voice was swallowed up by the sound of the music.

This wasn't right! I knew now what the whole Dingley Dell wedding was about.

Bunny didn't want to marry Uncle Max. Not really. She didn't love him. She just wanted Tarquin to take her back. That was why the wedding was exactly like the one they had planned together!

 My mind was whirling like a windmill as Bunny teetered towards a ring of polystyrene toadstools, where Uncle Max was

waiting to take her hand and promise to be her husband.

Instead of a vicar, a short fat man in a **hairy** orange suit stood underneath a plastic weeping willow tree. I think he was supposed to be some sort of woodland creature.

"Ladies and gentlemen," he announced in a thick, rolling voice, "here comes the bride!"

What was I going to do? How could I stop the wedding?

As Bunny walked, her train swished behind her like a dinosaur's tail. **THUMP!** I bounced from one side of the aisle to the other, clinging on for dear life. Between thumps, I caught sight of familiar faces sitting in the rows of tulip-shaped chairs.

THUMP! There was Nisha and her whole

family. They'd met Uncle Max lots of times at our house and, of course, when we held the sponsored jumpathon on their trampoline. THUMP! Then my mum and dad. THUMP! And ... Yana? What was she doing here? At first, I only caught sight of her green hair and thought it was a part of the Dingley Dell display – a giant spiky palm, perhaps. But it was definitely Yana. Her hair was extra tall and spiky for the wedding. She was wearing a gorgeous red dress covered in safety pins and a pair of amazing rainbow-striped tights.

THUMP! I supposed if Chip was here, it made sense that Yana was, too. THUMP! She must have met Max and Bunny when they came to PAW THINGS to adopt Chip. Yana had said the man was young and handsome ... that must have been Uncle Max!

Even though I knew I had to do something to stop the wedding, I felt another $tingle$ of excitement. Chip was here, all wrapped up in bows like the world's best present!

Bunny had slowed down now – her train stopped thrashing about.

Ahead of her, Uncle Max was dressed in a pale blue suit with a shirt and waistcoat almost as frilly as Bunny's dress. She had chosen his clothes for him, just like she had chosen the whole wedding.

As she stepped closer, I wriggled, trying to get free. But I was still caught in the frills of her dress, trapped like a fly in a STICKY WEB.

Uncle Max was chewing his lip nervously. I had never seen him look nervous before, not even on the video of him bungee jumping from the Grand Canyon.

"Please take a moment, ladies and gentlemen, to admire the wonders of nature," said the chubby woodland-creature-man in the hairy orange suit. He spread his arms to show the Dingley Dell.

But it wasn't nature – not really. It was all plastic and fake. Just like Bunny and this whole wedding.

I glanced around, peering out at the tinsel clouds, shiny polythene roses and. . .

"Lady Valance?" I gasped, spotting the judge from the dog show. What was she doing here, too? She was sitting right in the front row with an enormous new feathered hat. She was whispering something to a smart-looking gentleman with bushy white whiskers – probably her husband. Probably. . .

"Lord Valance!" I nearly choked on a mouthful of lace. Of course! Everything was starting to make sense. Bunny had said that Tarquin's father was a lord. And she said his mother would be wearing a feathery hat!

Sure enough, sitting on the other side of Lady Valance was a young man with wispy blond hair, a thin moustache and pale blue watery eyes . . . Tarquin! There was no doubt about it.

I was so busy staring at Tarquin – he was dressed in a frilly green suit the colour of lettuce – that it took me a moment to notice what the woodland-creature-man was saying.

"Ladies and gentlemen," he said, pointing to Uncle Max and Bunny as they stood before him. "If any person here can show cause why these two people should not be joined in marriage, speak now or forever hold your peace."

It was old-fashioned language, but I knew

at once what it meant. This was that moment in films where people always shout out and stop the marriage. It was the last chance for someone to say the wedding shouldn't go ahead. My last chance to say that I knew Bunny didn't really want to marry Uncle Max – that she was trying to make Tarquin jealous.

It seemed Bunny wanted to stop everything, too.

"Hasn't anybody got anything to say?" she asked, glancing hopefully at Tarquin.

The wedding guests all laughed. They thought it was a joke. Even Uncle Max laughed. But I knew the truth.

"Anyone?" said Bunny again. As I looked up from the frills of her dress, I could see there were tears in her eyes.

Tarquin wiped sweat from his lip with a pale green hankie.

The guests started to shift anxiously, realizing it might not be a joke.

"YES! I HAVE SOMETHING TO SAY!" I bellowed at the top of my tiny voice. I waved my arms. I didn't care if everybody saw how tiny I was – I couldn't let Uncle Max marry a woman who didn't love him.

"LISTEN TO ME, EVERYBODY!" I cried.

CHAPTER 23

"Did someone speak?" The woodland-creature-man who was leading the ceremony held up his hand.

"I don't think so." Lady Valance stood up from her seat in the front row. Her loud, clear voice boomed across the Dingley Dell. "It was just a dog. I heard it bark. Listen. . . There it goes again."

"RUFF!"

The door from the waiting room swung open and Chip came bounding in.

He must have escaped from the hamper. I had only pulled the lid shut, but never retied the ribbons.

He thundered down the aisle, yapping his head off.

"RUFF! RUFF! RUFF!"

He was barking wildly at the woodland-creature-man.

"Of course!" Now I saw what the man was supposed to be dressed up as: a squirrel.

"HELP!" The poor man leapt into a plastic

tree, looking even more like a squirrel than ever.

Wow! I have never seen one that big, I could imagine Chip saying to himself.

"That's Violet's dog," shouted Fifi-Belle as he almost knocked her over. "The one who stole my ice cream."

"Chip!" cried Nisha, jumping out of her chair.

"But where is Violet?" said Mum, standing up, too.

"I saw her coming in before," shrugged Tiff. "She's got to be here somewhere."

Now what should I do? I stood **frozen** to the spot. Should I climb out of the frills on Bunny's train and show myself, or should I stay hidden where I was?

Beside me, Uncle Max was talking to Fifi-Belle.

"But how can this be Violet's dog?" He tried to grab Chip by the collar. "I don't understand. I adopted him from **PAW THINGS**. That nice lady there – Yana – helped to settle him in. That's why I invited her to the wedding."

Now it was Yana's turn to stand.

"I did not know you were Violetta's uncle." Her Russian accent rang out from the back of the Dingley Dell. "Violetta looked after Chip sometimes. She will be so pleased to know he is going to a good home."

"But where is Violet?" yelled Mum. I think she was starting to panic.

"Oh dear." Just a few minutes earlier, while the ceremony was still going on, I had felt brave enough to leap out of Bunny's dress and show everyone how tiny I was. Anything if it meant stopping the wedding. But now I wasn't so sure.

The room was in uproar. Guests were talking. Chip was barking. The squirrel man was still swinging from the tree. Bunny was stamping her foot. Uncle Max was looking totally confused. And Mum was asking everyone if I they had any idea where I had gone.

Thanks to Chip, the wedding had stopped . . . at least for a while.

I smiled to myself. When suddenly. . .

WHOOSH!

There I was – back to FULL SIZE . . . flat on my back amongst the frills of Bunny's dress. I'd shot forward like a bullet when I grew. Now I was lying halfway under her big meringue skirt with my feet sticking out. Looking up, I could see Bunny's bloomers above me.

"Sorry," I spluttered, scrambling out from under her hem.

"**Ahhh!**" Bunny leapt in the air. "Violet? What are you doing down there?"

"Where have you been?" cried Mum.

"Erm ... I came in earlier," I said, pointing vaguely back towards the waiting room. "I just noticed a loose bow on the bottom of Bunny's dress. . ." I was hoping everyone had been too busy watching Chip and the squirrel man to actually see me shoot back to full size. "I thought I better mend it. Bridesmaid's duties, you know."

I reached out and straightened a crumpled bow. "There. That's better!"

"Get off me," flapped Bunny. "And take that horrible little dog out of here, too."

"Horrible?" I gasped.

"Horrible?" said Uncle Max. He was staring at Bunny with his mouth wide open.

"Yes," said Bunny. "Horrible! I have never seen such a silly-looking runt."

"It's not even purebred," agreed Tarquin, from his seat.

"I see," said Uncle Max. He had managed to catch hold of Chip at last. He passed him to me as the squirrel man slid gratefully out of his tree.

"Chip was supposed to be a wedding present," said Uncle Max. "A gift for you, Bunny."

"For me?" squealed Bunny.

"For her?" I gasped. It was silly, but somehow I'd still thought that Chip was meant for me. He'd been in the basket. In the waiting room. Where Bunny had said my present would be. There was nothing else there. Except . . . of course. . .

"The china shepherdess." I buried my head in Chip's fur. "That was my present. I should have guessed."

"Honestly, Max! How could you think I wanted a dog like that?" Bunny screeched. "Anyone who really knew me – anyone who really loved me would never have given me a scruffy little mongrel like that."

"I think Chip's cute," said Uncle Max. "That's why I chose him. He's a little naughty, but. . ."

"Er … excuse me," said the squirrel man. "Can we get on with the wedding now? We've got a Cheeky Cherub Christening at three o'clock."

" NO!" I cried. I had to do something. "You can't! I mean, you mustn't."

The room went silent. It was as if I had rung a loud dinner gong. Everyone was staring at me.

"Violet! Sit down," hissed Mum.

Dad patted the chair beside him.

I wished I could sit down. I wished I could hide away and shrink again. But I had to save Uncle Max. He had to know the truth about Bunny.

"I don't think the wedding should go on," I said, speaking as **loudly** and clearly as I could. My palms were sweating. "I don't think Bunny wants to marry Uncle Max. Not really."

There, I had said it.

"Bunny? Is this true?" Uncle Max spoke so quietly, I could hardly hear his voice at all.

"Oh . . . I don't know." Bunny squeezed out a tear. "I thought I loved you, Maxi. I really did. It's just that Tarquin and I planned to get married for so long. He understands me so well. . ."

"I've tried to be everything you want me to be," said Uncle Max.

"But Tarquin would never have given me a mangy little mutt like that. Would you, Tarqui?"

"Oh, Bunnykin," cried Tarquin, leaping from his chair. He flung his arms around Bunny. Or he tried to … but he couldn't reach round her **enormous** meringue dress.

"I would never have given you a scruffy stray from a rescue centre," he said. "I would have bought you a pedigree dog from the finest champion kennel. I've been such a fool. I should have stopped this wedding right from the start! I can't believe we ever broke up. And all because of a silly argument over what colour my handkerchiefs should be. I should never have let you go, Bunnykin. Never!"

"Ah … er … so," said the squirrel man, looking confused. "Do you still want me to carry on?"

"**NO!**" said Bunny and Uncle Max together. The guests gasped.

"This wedding is off," said Uncle Max, as

Chip leapt out of my arms and sat on a plastic toadstool scratching his ears. "I could never marry someone who turned away a stray just because he wasn't perfect or purebred." Uncle Max shook his head sadly. "We should be grateful to Chip ... and to Violet. She did something very brave – very responsible – when she spoke out today. You see, this is about more than a dog." Uncle Max loosened his bowtie. "I suppose I'm a bit like Chip, really," he said. "I'm just a happy, scruffy kind of person. But you tried to change me, Bunny. You tried to turn me into someone different ... yet you still didn't love me. You asked me to invite Tarquin as a guest at our wedding, but all along you wished he was the groom."

Uncle Max stepped forward as if he was going

to shake her hand. "I'm sorry, Bunny. We can never be husband and wife."

Chip leapt forward, too.

" **RUFF!** " He grabbed the hem of Bunny's dress in his teeth.

A few people laughed. But Uncle Max looked so sad I couldn't even smile. It was as if there was a big pink love heart that had been flashing inside him and now it had been turned off.

"Goodbye, Bunny," he whispered. "I hope Tarquin can make you happy."

And that was it. It was all over.

Except, when Bunny tried to leave with Tarquin, Chip played tug-of-war with the hem of her dress, shaking it like a huge dead swan. There was a terrible **ripping** sound . . . and Bunny was left standing in nothing but her vest and bloomers.

They were pale blue, of course ... and very, very **frilly**.

"Horrible little dog!" she screamed and she ran down the aisle, covering herself with Tarquin's green jacket and a bouquet of blue plastic roses.

CHAPTER 24

When all the other guests had gone home, my family stood in the car park at **WORLD OF WEDDINGS** with Uncle Max.

Yana waited a little to one side with Chip on a lead.

"I know it's tough, Max, but you did the right thing," said Dad, patting him on the back.

Uncle Max nodded. He stuffed the frilly bowtie into his pocket.

"What will you do now?" asked Mum.

"Where will you go?"

"You can stay with us for as long as you want," said Dad. "That would be lovely." Uncle Max put his arm around my shoulders. "But after that, in a few weeks, I think I'd like to travel. Go on one of my trips. Write a new book. Bunny wanted me to stay home and work in an office, but ..." Uncle Max shook his head. "... that's just not really me."

"But what about Chip?" I said, glancing over at Yana. "He can't go travelling with you."

Chip heard his name and tugged Yana closer.

"True," said Uncle Max, bending down to stroke Chip's ears. "I have to look after this little guy now. I can't just go trotting off whenever I feel like it."

"But you must go travelling," said Mum. "You're never happier than when you're crawling through some snake-infested swamp or jumping out of some rickety old aeroplane." She bent down and stroked Chip's other ear. "I know it is hard. But perhaps it is best if Chip goes back to PAW THINGS. He seems very fond of Yana, so—"

"But I am leaving," Yana interrupted. "In two weeks. I am going to Siberia to work with wolves in the wild."

"Siberia?" said Uncle Max. "Wild wolves? That sounds fascinating." There was a twinkle in his eye I hadn't seen for a long time. "I did some research when Violet and I adopted Boris, the wolf cub. I've always thought a book about the wolves and why they're endangered could help raise a lot of money."

"Certainly," agreed Yana. "It would be a fantastic help to the project."

"But Chip can't go back to PAW THINGS," I said. "Not without you there, Yana."

"He will miss me, it is true," said Yana. "He likes the other workers there, but. . ."

"But you're special to him," I said.

Yana nodded. "And you are special to him too, Violetta."

"But don't you see? That would be perfect!" said Uncle Max, turning to Mum. "Chip wouldn't have to go back to *PAW THINGS*. Not if I knew Violet could look after him for me. Just sometimes? When I am away on long trips."

"Oh please, Mum," I cried, scooping Chip up in my arms.

Mum looked at me. She looked at Chip. She looked at Uncle Max. She looked at Dad and she looked at Tiffany.

Then she looked at Chip again and sighed.

"Oh, I suppose so," she said. "Poor little thing . . . he does deserve a family."

" *DEFINITELY!* " I cried. "Thank you! Thank you! Thank you!" I flung my arms around

Mum's neck as Chip joined in the hug and nibbled her nose.

"That is so unfair," said Tiffany. "I can't believe Violet is getting a dog."

"She's not getting a dog," said Mum. "She's just borrowing one. When Uncle Max is away."

"But you said I could get hair straighteners," Tiffany sulked.

"Perhaps you can borrow some of those from somewhere, too," giggled Dad, looking at Tiff's sunflower hair.

"Bunny left something like that in my flat," said Uncle Max. "Really fancy ones. But I have a feeling she won't be coming back for them. You can borrow those, if you like."

"Seriously?" grinned Tiffany.

"Seriously," said Uncle Max.

As we walked towards the car, he whispered in my ear, "You might be able to borrow Chip for a very long time, if we play our cards right."

"Really?" I said, my mouth dry with excitement.

"Yes." Uncle Max smiled – a proper smile that spread right across his face. "I mean it about this trip to Siberia. Especially if Yana thinks a book would be helpful. I'd LOVE to live with the wolves. Perhaps I'll even meet Boris. And I know you'll always look after Chip."

"Always," I said, my heart beating against Chip's shaggy fur as I held him in my arms. "Just one thing, Uncle Max. How do you spell Siberia?"

"S-I-B-E-R-I-A. It's a cold, snowy state in the east of Russia," said Uncle Max. "But why do you want to know how to spell it? Are you going to send me a postcard?"

"Maybe," I said, muttering the letters under my breath. "I like to spell whenever I'm excited. It helps me stay calm. . .

"S-I-B-E-R-I-A."
"S-I-B-E-R-I-A."

I repeated the letters over and over again.

I couldn't believe it. Chip was coming home with me. He was coming to stay.

Three weeks later, Nisha and I were sitting in my lounge. It was spinach stew for supper. But I didn't care. Chip was here.

Everything was perfect. Well, everything except for the spinach, of course. And I did still owe Ratty-Riley a MOUNTAIN of TOFFAMEL bars. And I was still paying Mum back for the lost wellie boot. And Miss Penman had given us HEAPS of

~~turrifically tuff speelings~~ terrifically tough spellings to learn for the holidays. <u>And</u> I was still a bit wobbly on my seven times tables. But, I didn't care about any of that any more. Not now that I had Chip to look after.

He was lying on my lap, exhausted from a long walk in the park.

While I stroked him, Nisha groomed his ears. She brushed and brushed till they shone like bronze.

"He almost looks smart," laughed Mum peeping in from the hall. "Here you are, Violet. A postcard came from Uncle Max."

"FANTASTIC!" I cried as Mum handed me a snowy picture of a wolf. Chip jumped off the chair and followed her to the kitchen as she went to finish cooking the spinach stew. Chip loves spinach. He gobbles up all the scraps ... just like I always said he would.

"Read the postcard out loud," said Nisha.

"OK." I turned it over.

Hi there, Violet and Chip!
Siberia is super-cool (and I don't just mean cold).

Chip - you would love the funny long-eared squirrels we get here. And Violet would love the huskies and the wolves.

Yana and I went snow trekking with the dogs for four days last week. We found a wolf pack and followed them north into the mountains. We made camp in the woods and slept close to the fire to keep warm. It was too cold to wash and we had to boil snow to make tea.

More soon —
Love from Uncle Max

And Yana x

Miss V

25 K

Swa

Nor

Er

S

"I wish I was there! Think how exciting it would be to follow the wolves and camp near an open fire," I said. "I can just see Uncle Max and Yana listening to the howling and staring up at the stars."

"How romantic," giggled Nisha.

"Yes, isn't it?" I said. And I felt a sudden fizzy tingling in my toes.

WHOOSH!

"Not again! Honestly, Violet," laughed Nisha as I shrank right before her eyes. "What's so exciting now?"

"Imagine if Uncle Max and Yana fall in love and get married," I cried, grabbing hold of the postcard and floating to the floor as if I were riding a magic carpet. "That's one wedding I would **DEFINITELY** LOVE to be a bridesmaid for!"

Acknowledgements

Huge thanks to Alice Swan and all the team at Scholastic for being TOTALLY brilliant – especially Alison Padley for her crazy fonts and FUN design. To Kirsten Collier for the wonderful illustrations. Also Pat White and Claire Wilson at RCW for looking after me so well. And to Sophie McKenzie for yet more TERRIFIC advice. Thanks to my friends and family too, and to Willesden the dog, who snoozed by my feet while I wrote this book.

LOOK OUT
for Violet's other adventures

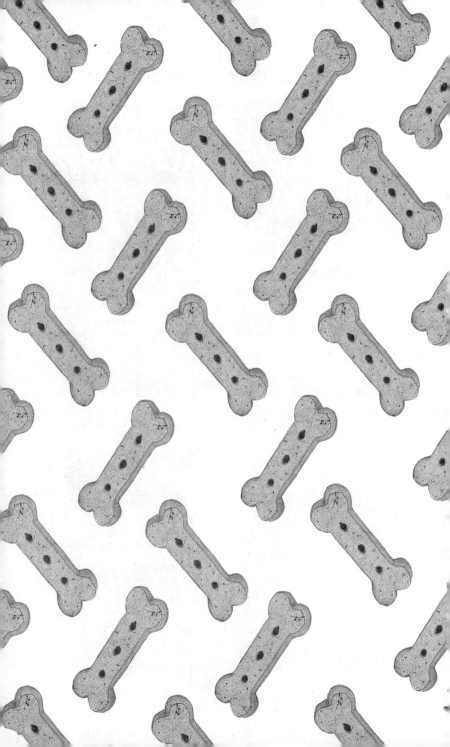